"Your dark eyes hold the ocean, your voice is birds in flight," Billy sang, his voice filled with longing. "I'd like to see the moonlight kiss your velvet skin tonight . . ."

Carrie's eyes darted again to Kristy. A triumphant grin was etched across her face. There was certainly no doubt in Kristy's mind about whom the song was intended for.

A hot tingle tickled Carrie's nose. *No crying!* she told herself. *I forbid you to cry.* The tingle subsided and Carrie regained control of herself. *So this is what it means to be crazy about someone*, she thought despondently. *I must've been crazy to ever think I'd stand a chance.*

Coming soon
in the SUNSET ISLAND
series

Sunset Dreams
Sunset Farewell

Don't miss

Sunset Island

Sunset Kiss

Cherie Bennett

A BERKLEY / SPLASH BOOK

SUNSET KISS is an original publication
of The Berkley Publishing Group.
This work has never appeared before in book form.

A Berkley Book / published by arrangement with
General Licensing Company, Inc.

PRINTING HISTORY
Berkley edition / July 1991

A GLC BOOK

ISBN: 0-425-12899-7

A BERKLEY BOOK ® TM 757,375
Berkley Books are published by The Berkley Publishing Group,
200 Madison Avenue, New York, New York 10016.

PRINTED IN THE UNITED STATES OF AMERICA

10 9 8 7 6 5 4 3 2 1

Sunset Kiss

ONE

"Is this the coolest, or what?" Carrie Alden asked as she stood backstage at the Sunset Island Arts Pavilion.

"This is beyond cool," laughed Sam Bridges, tossing back her wild red mane. "It's like some kind of unreal MTV dream. I always knew my first summer out of high school would be a blast, but this summer is turning out to be even more amazing than I imagined."

Carrie smiled at her friend. She was right. This did seem like some kind of wonderful dream. A mere three weeks before, she would never have expected to be backstage at a Graham Perry concert—as Graham Perry's personal guest!

On every side of her, people worked feverishly. The sound system was being checked and the lights adjusted, instruments were being tuned and retuned. The energy level was so high! Carrie felt that if she reached out, she might actually feel the air crackle with electricity.

"Ooh! Ooh!" Sam jabbed Carrie's shoulder. "You're missing a hot photo op."

Carrie's hands flew to the camera she wore around her neck. It wasn't every day an aspiring photographer got backstage passes to a Graham Perry concert. Carrie was determined to make the most of the opportunity. Maybe she'd even get shots good enough to sell to *Rolling Stone.*

Following Sam's gaze, Carrie focused her camera. This *was* a great shot. Graham stood just offstage, going over some notes with his band. The amber overhead light threw dramatic shadows on the rock superstar's handsome face. His expression was concentrated, intense—not the usual easygoing, smiling face he showed to the public. It revealed the demanding professional beneath the casual it's-so-easy façade. And Carrie was talented enough to know instinctively that photography was more than mere image. A great photographer used the camera to unveil the hidden truth lurking just beneath the surface of the image.

Carrie composed the shot and then snapped quickly, shooting from three slightly different angles. "That's going to be a really interesting photo of Graham!" she said. "Thanks for pointing it out. You have a terrific eye."

"No, no, noooooo!" Sam chided. "I wasn't talking about Graham. You already have a zillion pictures of him. I was talking about *that* picture." Sam pointed onstage to where the warmup band, Flirting with Danger, was already set up. With their backs to the girls, the lead singer, Billy

Sampson, and the bass guitarist, Presley Travis, were deep in conversation.

Sam touched her thumbs together and framed out the picture for Carrie. "I even know what you could call this photo. 'Hot Buns in Conference.'"

"Sam! You are so *bad*," Carrie said as she snapped the photo.

"Maybe, but you did take the picture, didn't you?" Sam teased.

"What I'm doing is sort of a photographic essay," Carrie said carefully. "The warmup band is part of the story, too."

"Yeah, right," Sam told her. "It couldn't be that you'd like to do some flirting of your own with the lead singer. Oh no." Sam snorted.

Carrie tried to look casual, but couldn't help the faint blush that rose in her face. "Like the kind of flirting you do with Presley?" she said. "No way. I could never be so bold."

"Don't worry, I'll be happy to give you lessons," Sam said. "This summer is as good a time as any for you to come out of that demure shell and be all the vixen you can be."

"Oh, Sam," Carrie said, laughing. "You never give up." Still, she thought to herself, Sam's remarks had hit home. Her interest in Flirting with Danger was more than just professional.

Flirting with Danger was a local band on the island. Opening for Graham Perry that night might turn out to be their big break. The guys were nervous and exhilarated at the same time. They wanted to be sure everything was perfect.

"There must be music big shots in the audience tonight," Sam speculated. "All those honchos vacation around here. I'm sure they wouldn't miss their god, Graham Perry. Maybe one of them will pick up on the Flirts."

"That would be great," Carrie agreed. "When they're big stars we can say we knew them when they were just a local band."

"Yeah, and we'll have standing invitations backstage. We'll go everywhere they go. Our pictures will be in *People*. We'll be famous, too," Sam said excitedly.

"Sam, we don't even know them very well," Carrie pointed out.

"Well, we'll just have to work on getting to know them better, won't we?" Sam said confidently. That was one of the things Carrie admired about her friend. To Sam everything seemed simple. If you wanted something, you went after it. Simple.

Sam and Carrie knew Billy and Pres from around the island, though they'd met them only recently. Still, Pres had most definitely flirted back with Sam the last time they met. And Carrie knew Billy liked her. He'd even lent her the camera she was using that night, his new Canon EOS-1. She was sure he wouldn't have done that for just anyone. What she didn't know was whether he liked her as a friend or if the attraction went deeper.

There was one thing Carrie *did* know: Billy Sampson turned her on. She'd felt it the minute they'd met in front of Wheels, the bike and moped rental shop. Partly, it was his looks. He was tall, with long, sun-streaked, sandy blond hair, which he wore tied back in a ponytail, and big, soulful brown eyes. One ear was pierced with a small silver crescent-moon earring.

It was his looks that attracted her, but there was something else, too. Carrie had felt an immediate connection to Billy. It was hard to explain. It was definitely what people meant by "chemistry."

As if he felt her watching him, Billy turned and looked toward Carrie. For a moment their eyes locked, and it was like a touch. A touch that sent an electrifying tingle through Carrie's entire body.

Then the moment was gone.

Billy smiled and waved. Carrie waved back. *Did he feel that?* Carrie wondered. *Or is it just me?* The connection seemed so real to her. He had to feel it, too.

At that moment a stunning blond girl in a red leather mini and matching short-cropped jacket joined Carrie and Sam. Sam stepped back and appraised the outfit. "All *right!* Princess Grace breaks out the red leather for the big night!" she cheered. "Way to go, Emma!"

Emma Cresswell blushed. "I figured if I'm ever going to wear this outfit again, tonight's the night. And stop calling me Princess Grace."

"Why? She was beautiful, and you look just like her. Did you ever see that Hitchcock movie, *Rear*

Window? Grace Kelly had such gorgeous clothes in that. It's, like, this ancient movie, but her clothes would be in style today. Weird." Sam's large blue eyes narrowed in thought for a moment. "I don't think Grace would have worn red leather, though."

"Good," said Emma, lifting her delicate chin defiantly. "I don't want to look like Grace Kelly. I'm dumping the designer royalty look forever. From now on I'm burning."

"You're supposed to say *burrrnin'* with kind of a sexy growl, not *burning* as in 'Jeeves, I believe the chateau is burning down,'" Sam corrected her friend.

Emma's blue eyes went wide. "How did you know our butler's name is Jeeves? I don't remember telling you guys that."

"I was kidding," replied Sam. "Jeeves is the name of the butler in practically every old movie."

"Are you joking?" Carrie asked Emma incredulously. "Tell me you don't really have a butler named Jeeves."

"Sorry," said Emma with a rueful smile. "But that really is his name. Anyway, to change the subject—*please, please* let's change the subject—you ladies look extremely sizzling tonight yourselves."

Sam spread her long arms wide to show off her black T-shirt dress. The sleeves had been cut into strips at the top of the arm. The strips were then beaded and knotted into fringe that fell from each sleeve. The same knotted, beaded fringe fell from the short hemline. With her characteristic flair for fashion, Sam had belted the dress with an Indian-beaded belt that showed off her slender waist to full advantage.

"Do you like it?" she asked. "The monsters and I sat on the porch last night and each made ourselves one. We cut the fringe, put the beads on, everything. Of course, mine came out much better than theirs did." The "monsters" were Becky and Allie Jacobs, thirteen-year-old identical twins whom Sam was taking care of this summer. "It doesn't look tacky or anything, does it?" Sam questioned, her brash, self-assured demeanor fading for just a moment.

"You look fabulous, as always," said Emma. Five feet ten inches and willowy, Sam rarely looked anything less than spectacular in whatever she wore. Her long, curly red hair and her beautiful, perfectly made-up face made Sam a knockout.

"Forget it," scoffed Carrie. "I'm not standing next to you guys anymore. I *would* have to pick two beauty queens to be my best friends. Good going, Carrie."

"Get off it," said Sam. "You are seriously adorable and you know it. Or at least you should. And if I could just get the teeniest little bit of makeup on that Ivory-girl face, you'd have every guy on this island falling down stone dead in his tracks."

"No thanks. That's not me," said Carrie lightly.

"Besides, I wouldn't want to have to step over all those dead bodies." Despite her joking manner, Carrie did hope she looked good that night. She'd combed out her long chestnut-brown hair until it shone and worn her best hammered-silver hoop earrings. She was wearing a calf-length, yellow-and-blue striped pinafore jumper over a yellow T-shirt with rolled sleeves. She'd liked the outfit when she put it on. Now she wondered if it looked babyish. "Does this really look okay?" she asked.

"It's summery and casual, but pretty. It's very you," Emma assured her. "You look like you've lived on Sunset Island all your life."

"Thanks," said Carrie, turning back to watch the frenetic activity all around her.

"Let's see if we recognize anyone in the audience," Emma suggested. The girls walked to the front of the stage and parted the thick velvet curtains. The seats were filling up rapidly. "There are the Hewitts," said Emma, spotting Jane and Jeff Hewitt, the husband-and-wife law partners she worked for. "They seem so, you know, old to me. It's odd to think of them liking rock and roll."

"I'll bet Graham Perry is somewhere around their age," Carrie reminded Emma.

"That's unbelievable," said Sam, shaking her head as though this was somehow sad news.

Unbelievable, Carrie echoed in her thoughts as she gazed out at the throng of people taking their seats. Yes, that was a pretty good word to describe all that had happened since they'd arrived on chic Sunset Island to work as au pairs for some of the wealthy families who vacationed there.

The first completely unbelievable thing was that Carrie had been hired by the Templetons—as in Claudia and Graham Perry Templeton. It turned out that Templeton was Graham Perry's real last name but Carrie hadn't known who her employers really were until she arrived on the island. Mr. Rudolph, the Templetons' business manager, had hired her at the au pair convention in New York.

The convention was actually a big weekend meeting held at a hotel. During the weekend, girls who wanted summer jobs as mother's helpers—also known as au pairs—had met prospective employers from all around the country. It was there that Carrie had been interviewed and hired by Mr. Rudolph. Now Carrie was living in a fabulous mansion, taking care of the rock star's two adorable children, and having the summer of her life.

The second unbelievably great thing to happen had also begun back at the au pair convention. Carrie had met Sam and Emma there. They'd become fast friends, deciding that they wanted to work together on gorgeous, beachy Sunset Island. Luckily all three of them had been hired to work on the island. And in the two weeks since they had arrived, their friendship had really grown.

There had been a few hurdles. One major one, really. Just the week before, Sam and Carrie had discovered Emma's secret, which she'd been desperately trying to hide with a complicated web of lies and half-truths. Of course, when the secret is that you're one of the megarich and famous Boston Cresswells, it's kind of hard to hide it. Especially when a snotty rich girl on the island is determined to expose you. Discover your secret. Lorell Courtland had hounded Emma from the minute she'd arrived, finally importing the meanest, snobbiest girl from Emma's boarding school to unmask Emma in front of her new-found friends. That had been a pretty ugly scene.

For a while Carrie and Sam had felt betrayed. Why had Emma lied to them? Did they really know her at all? But after Emma had explained how she was hoping to find herself—or at least redefine herself—without the trappings of her parents' money and status, they forgave her. Emma had been truly contrite and there was no question that, aside from her amazing background, she was one of the nicest people around. No wonder she'd run like the blazes to get away from her family and all the snobby creeps like Lorell she'd been surrounded with all her life. Now the threesome was back together and ready to "rave on," as Sam liked to say.

And now this, probably the *most* unbelievable thing. Taking pictures at a Graham Perry concert! Backstage! Just before coming to the island, Carrie had won second prize in the New Jersey State Teen Photographers Contest. She'd thought nothing could top that. But as far as she was concerned, this was even more thrilling.

"Look," said Sam, "isn't that the barracuda we saw at Howie Lawrence's party?" Sam was looking in the direction of a long-legged young woman of about twenty with shoulder-length, shaggy blond hair.

"Yeah," said Carrie. "She's the one who was all over Billy. What's she doing here?"

"I don't know, but she's talking to Graham Perry's drummer and recording everything he says," noted Emma.

"Maybe she'll hit on him and leave Billy alone tonight," Carrie suggested hopefully.

"Speaking of incredible hunks, I do believe Billy is approaching," whispered Sam. "And so is his awesome companion, Pres."

Sure enough, Billy and Pres were walking toward them. *Quiet!* Carrie commanded her heart, which had suddenly started beating like a jackhammer at top speed. *Be cool*, she ordered herself sternly.

"*Hola*, vixens. *Qué tal?*" Pres greeted them in his sultry Southern voice.

"We vixens *qué tal* just fine," laughed Sam flirtatiously.

How does she do it? Carrie wondered. *Maybe in order to flirt so easily, you have to be born that way. In that case, I may as well just give up now.*

Carrie raised her eyes and realized with a start that Billy was standing inches from her side. She smiled to cover her nervousness, and he grinned back. The easy banter going on between Sam and Pres continued, but Carrie wasn't paying attention.

"Hi," she said. *I am so dull!* she thought furiously.

Billy reached out a hand toward Carrie and for one crazy, paralyzing moment she wondered if he was going to touch her breasts. Instead he touched the camera slung around her neck. *Get a grip on yourself!* Carrie counseled herself silently.

"How are you doing with that camera?"

"It's great," Carrie replied sincerely. "It practically does all the work for you. Thanks for letting me use it."

"No problem. But remember, we made a deal. You get to use the camera in exchange for giving me some photography lessons. I'm all thumbs with that thing."

"You'll pick it up quickly," said Carrie, glad to be talking about photography. At least it was a conversation she could feel comfortable with. "And I can show you anything else you need to do."

"I'm sure you can," he said in a tone that implied he might not be talking about the camera anymore. His voice and the way his dark eyes took her in sent a delicious warmth coursing through her body. She met his gaze, and again she felt that wordless communication.

Carrie was so wrapped up in Billy that she hadn't noticed the approach of the blonde who'd been interviewing Graham Perry's drummer. But now the sexy young woman stood right between Billy and Pres.

Up close she didn't look as naturally gorgeous as she had from a distance. Still, she exuded sexuality. Her hazel eyes were narrow despite their halo of heavy makeup and she had a sensual, too-wide mouth, which was painted a vivid red. She was slim and very obviously braless beneath her soft, clingy peach T-shirt. "Okay, Flirts, it's your turn," she said to the guys, completely ignoring Sam, Carrie, and Emma.

"Hey, Kristy," said Pres. "Are you going to make us famous?"

"Sure am," Kristy cooed. She placed one hand on Billy's shoulder and leaned so close that her hair brushed his lips. "Sorry, darling," she said, pulling back as she picked at an invisible piece of lint on his black T-shirt. She didn't let go of Billy's shoulder, though.

Billy gently disengaged her fingers. "Kristy, I'd like you to meet Carrie, Sam, and Emma," he said pleasantly.

Kristy shot them a quick, insincere smile. "How nice," she said, barely shifting her gaze. "I'm sure you *girls* will excuse us, but we need privacy. I'd love to see your dressing room." She directed this last remark at Pres and Billy.

Pres looked amused, but also as if he was loving every minute of it. Billy was harder to read.

"Kristy writes the 'Around Town' column for

the *Breakers*," he explained, naming Sunset Island's one and only newspaper.

"Oh yes, I've read your column," Emma said politely.

"Oh yes, everyone does," Kristy answered without the slightest attempt at modesty.

Billy looked at Carrie, laughter in his eyes. Was he laughing at Kristy? Carrie couldn't tell. "I guess we'd better go do this interview," he said. "We struggling musicians need all the exposure we can get."

Kristy walked her long fingernails down Billy's muscled arm. "Stick with me and I'll give you all the exposure you want," she purred.

"Well, then, let's go do it right now," said Pres. "We have to go on in about five minutes, so let's just stay close to the stage, okay?"

"See you after we play, ladies," said Billy, letting Kristy drag him away.

"Can you believe she thinks everyone reads her column?" Carrie asked once they were by themselves. "I mean, Sunset Island is hardly the media capital of the world."

"You were expecting modesty from someone in an outfit like that?" Sam asked.

"She's got a big ego, all right," Emma agreed.

"I wasn't talking about the size of her ego," Sam said pointedly.

"Do you think she's attractive?" Carrie wanted to know. The easy way Kristy had draped herself all over Billy bothered her more than she could admit, even to her friends.

"In a trashy way, I suppose," Emma conceded, wrinkling her nose daintily.

"Trashy!" Sam yelped. "Trashy is being kind. Try slut queen supreme. I mean, she might as well be topless. It's kind of impossible for a guy not to notice that. Hey, I could get guys to look at me, too, if I just took off my shirt."

Sam grabbed at her T-shirt dress, and for a moment Carrie thought she was about to demonstrate her point. "Whoa! Down, girl," Carrie said, laughing despite herself. "We don't want you hauled out of here for indecent exposure."

"They should haul off that Kristy for indecent everything," Emma said loyally.

Carrie tried not to stare as Kristy interviewed the band in an alcove just offstage. But it was hard not to. Kristy had perched herself on Billy's knee. And while Billy didn't seem to be playing up to her, he wasn't bumping her off his knee, either.

Suddenly Carrie felt horribly sick. Her stomach churned and a general feeling of anxiety washed over her. *What a stupid twerp I am,* she derided herself miserably. *Why would Billy be interested in me when he has the Kristys of the world throwing themselves at him? Next to someone like that I look like some kind of overgrown Girl Scout.*

"Don't let that man-eater get to you," Emma told her gently.

"Does it show?" asked Carrie.

"It's written all over your face," Sam confirmed.

"She *is* more his age," argued Carrie.

"Oh, bull," Sam said. "Where true love—not to mention true sex—is concerned, there is no such thing as the right age."

"Easy for you to say," Carrie murmured, unconvinced. She'd felt so young and gawky next to smooth, sexy Kristy.

Just then the backstage lights dimmed and spotlights illuminated the stage. Flirting with Danger sauntered to the wings. Jon Hess, the man in charge of the Arts Pavilion, went out to the center microphone. "And now, without further delay, here is Flirting with Danger!" he shouted.

The band members ran onstage amid enthusiastic applause and screams. They had a huge local following and all their biggest fans were in the audience that night. They launched into a rousing, rocking tune, an original song called "Say What? U Lie," and had the crowd whipped up into a frenzy in seconds.

Before this, Carrie had only heard their demo tape. A friend named Howie Lawrence (who really wanted to be more than just a friend) had played it at a party. She'd liked their music then, but, seeing them live was an entirely different thing. They were explosive. Exciting. Sexy. Especially Billy.

"Who does he sound like?" asked Sam, who was

gyrating to the music as she spoke. "He sounds like somebody."

"Jon Bon Jovi?" suggested Emma.

"A little, maybe," said Sam, "but I'm thinking of someone else. He sounds almost exactly like somebody else."

"I know," said Carrie. "He sounds like that guy from that old group. The one who died."

"Jim Morrison!" Emma recalled the name. "My Aunt Liz has all the old Doors albums. She's a major Doors fan. You're right. That's exactly who he sounds like."

Carrie sighed. Hearing Billy sing had just put him right over the top on her personal sex-appeal register. Before he sang he'd been a nine. Now he was a ten and a half. She closed her eyes and let his deep voice fill her senses. He had a voice full of experience. It was knowing, a little sad, and loaded with sexual energy.

The song ended. Carrie opened her eyes dreamily.

"Oh, this girl has it bad," teased Sam. "You should see your face, Carrie."

Billy spoke into the microphone. "This next song is dedicated to a real lovely lady who's backstage tonight." The band then went into a slow, romantic warmup. "This is one of our original songs and it's called 'Before the First Kiss,'" Billy told the audience over the music.

"Yesssss! Yessssss!" Sam hissed, poking Carrie sharply. "Your love vibes are being returned! This is great!"

"He doesn't mean me," replied Carrie darkly.

"Sure he does," said Emma. "It's got to be you."

"Oh, yeah? Look at that." Carrie jerked her head, gesturing to a spot over near the curtain. There stood Kristy Powell, her arms wrapped across her chest, swaying seductively to the music. Her eyes were closed and she wore a blissful expression. "This song is meant for her," said Carrie.

"She obviously thinks so," noted Emma. "But she's wrong. Who would ever describe her as a lovely lady?"

"Billy," muttered Carrie.

"Be quiet," scolded Sam. "This is the most romantic thing that could happen to you and you're talking through it. Shut up and listen to the song. It's meant for you. Forget her."

"Your dark eyes hold the ocean, your voice is birds in flight," Billy sang, his voice filled with longing. "I'd like to see the moonlight kiss your velvet skin tonight . . ."

Carrie's eyes darted again to Kristy. A triumphant grin was etched across her face. There was certainly no doubt in Kristy's mind about whom the song was intended for.

A hot tingle tickled Carrie's nose. *No crying!* she told herself. *I forbid you to cry.* The tingle subsided and Carrie regained control of herself. *So this is what it means to be crazy about someone*, she thought despondently. *I must've been crazy to ever think I'd stand a chance.*

TWO

Onstage, Graham Perry sang a string of the hits that had made him a rock legend. The concert was into its second hour, but the time had passed quickly for Carrie. With steely determination, she'd managed to put Billy out of her mind and to concentrate on the show. After taking a few performance photos, she joined Emma and Sam, who were settled on folding chairs in the stage wings.

Normally, rock wasn't even Carrie's favorite music. In their junior year of high school, her ex-boyfriend, Josh, had become very interested in jazz. His enthusiasm was catching and soon he and Carrie listened to nothing but jazz. They had gone to jazz concerts, listened to jazz stations, even made spring trips to Manhattan to browse through record stores for rare jazz records.

But jazz was nonexistent on Sunset Island. The clubs played rock and the town sponsored classical concerts. She couldn't even tune in a jazz station. Surprisingly, she had discovered she was glad. Jazz had been a thing she shared with Josh.

Now that they'd broken up, she realized that Josh had formed lots of her opinions and tastes. He was so intelligent that she'd always assumed that whatever he liked was superior to anything else.

Now Josh wasn't her constant companion anymore, though they still wrote. Part of her goal in getting away this summer was to find out who she was without Josh. And maybe learning to like rock was a part of it. She had found that without Josh there telling her rock was loud and stupid, she *did* like it.

She was sitting forward in her chair, thinking about Josh and swaying in time to the music, when suddenly she felt a touch at her shoulder. It was Billy. "You were great," she whispered as he crouched down beside her chair.

"Thanks. I feel real good. It was definitely one of our better nights," he replied, smiling. This was the first time Carrie had seen him since the band finished playing. The crowd had roared its applause, but as soon as the intermission lights came up, Billy had been demoted from rock star to roadie. Unlike Graham Perry, who worked with an entourage of technicians, Flirting with Danger had to break down and load its own equipment.

"Listen, Pres and I decided to have some people back to the house after the concert. Are you ladies free?" Billy asked.

"I am," said Sam.

"Me, too," agreed Emma.

Carrie's heart sank. "Not me," she said. "Graham and Claudia hired a sitter so I'd be free for the concert, but she's just thirteen and can't stay out past eleven. I have to get back and relieve her."

"Too bad," said Billy, looking sincerely disappointed. "Why don't you try to talk Graham into giving you the night off? He's kind of an old guy; maybe he'll be tired after the concert and change his mind about going out."

"I'll try," said Carrie. "But I'm not counting on it. Graham and Claudia are real party animals."

"Give it a shot, anyway," Billy pressed. He turned to Sam and Emma. "Pres and I share a house with some other guys over on Dune Road. You can't miss it. It's the one with the neon-purple front porch."

"It sounds divine," said Sam drily.

"We didn't paint it, we just rented it," Billy laughed. "It *is* my favorite thing about the house, though." Billy got to his feet and checked over his shoulder. "I'd better help them finish loading the van. Maybe I'll see you all later."

"Do you think you can get off?" Sam asked eagerly once Billy was gone.

"Not a chance," said Carrie.

The rest of the concert dragged for Carrie. Graham was terrific, but she wasn't really listening. All she could think about was Kristy and Billy being together at the party. Kristy had gone out into the audience, but Carrie was pretty sure she'd be at the party. She seemed to show up everywhere.

Carrie had been to enough Sunset Island parties to know that the bedrooms very quickly became occupied with amorous couples. Was tonight the night Kristy would snag Billy by dragging him off to one of those rooms? On the other hand, that might happen even if Carrie was there. And that would be much worse.

Still, it wasn't fair. The one complaint Carrie had about Graham and Claudia was that they went out a lot. And they always expected her to be on call, even if they decided to go out at the last possible minute. It wasn't something she felt she could talk to them about. After all, it was the reason they'd hired her. Mr. Rudolph had made that very clear at the interview. "Oh, that's no problem at all," she'd told him eagerly. Back then she'd had no idea that Sunset Island would offer so many fun things to do at night—fun things that she now minded missing.

After Graham did two encores, the house lights finally came up. Drenched with sweat but elated, Graham walked into the wings with the rest of his band.

His wife, Claudia, joined him. She stood with her arm around her husband as he greeted VIPs who'd come backstage to say hello. They made a handsome couple. Graham, who was in his late thirties, was tall and lanky, with a head of thick, wavy brown hair which he wore long in the back. Only up close could you see that it was shot through with gray. His face was lined but still handsome. He'd been a rock superstar for close to twenty years. It was not an easy life, yet Graham seemed supremely confident and at ease in it.

Claudia was his second wife. At twenty-five, she seemed much more poised than her years. Carrie sometimes wondered if Claudia had been a gypsy in another life. Her style was all fringed shawls, gauzy skirts, jangly jewelry, and batik scarves. Yet she never looked raggedy. Just the opposite. She always looked gorgeous.

"Of course she does," Sam had noted. "Every little belt and bracelet she wears comes from some ritzy European boutique and costs more than my whole wardrobe."

Despite their demanding social schedule, Carrie liked Claudia and Graham. They were a nice couple and treated her very well. They never questioned where she went or asked her to be in at a specific time. Giving her and two friends backstage passes was just one of the many nice things they'd done for her.

"Hi there," came a familiar voice from behind Carrie. It was Howie Lawrence.

"Hi," Carrie greeted the short, slightly built, bespectacled nineteen-year-old. Though Howie didn't interest Carrie romantically, she did like him. Respected him, even. Howie's family was extremely wealthy, but Howie was unpretentious. He spent his spare time doing volunteer work with learning-disabled kids, and Carrie admired that. She'd sort of dated him a couple of times but there was no attraction. At least not on her part. Unfortunately for both of them, Howie was extremely smitten and trailed Carrie like a puppy dog.

"Are you here with your father?" asked Emma. Howie's father was a top executive with Polyphonic Records, Graham's recording label.

Howie nodded. "Yeah. Dad's having Graham and Claudia and some press people and execs over to the house. I'd invite you, but it's hotshots only tonight."

"Oh, well, excuse us," pouted Sam, pretending to be offended. "I thought we *were* hotshots. I mean, if we don't rate with you, then—"

"I didn't mean that. I mean, of course you're hotshots . . . to me, that is. I didn't mean to imply otherwise, but . . . " Howie stammered helplessly.

"Don't worry about it, Howie," Carrie interrupted. "She's just busting your chops. I have to go home anyway, and they already have a party to go to."

"I'm not going," said Emma. "I wouldn't feel right if you're not going, Carrie."

"You're not going?" asked Sam, disappointed. "I guess I won't go then, either."

"Don't stay home because of me," Carrie urged them. "If you go, you can give me the full report."

"No," said Sam glumly. "Emma's right. It wouldn't be fun without you."

At that moment Claudia joined them. Her long, permed blond hair fell around her shoulders. She wore an exquisite dress that seemed to be made entirely of patterned scarves stitched together with golden thread. "Did you enjoy the concert?" she asked the girls and Howie.

"It was completely amazing," said Sam. "Thanks again for the passes. I'll never forget this."

"Me either," Emma agreed. "Thanks."

"It was my pleasure," Claudia replied. "Okay, Carrie, now we have to scoot you home. I can't believe I left my twelve-year-old stepson with a thirteen-year-old babysitter. As we left, I think he was trying to date her."

"Knowing Ian, he's probably succeeded," Carrie chuckled. "That kid can really turn on the charm."

"I know what you mean. Let's get you home, and fast," said Claudia. "Has anyone got the number for a car service?"

"Don't worry about it. I already have a car coming," Emma volunteered. "We can drop Carrie off."

"Great, see you later," said Claudia, heading back toward her husband.

Carrie waved. "Thanks again, Claudia." She turned to Emma with a twinkle in her eyes. "So you now have a car service at your beck and call, eh? I guess things are totally back on track with you and Kurt."

Emma's pretty face turned radiant. "Oh, yes, things with Kurt and me are great. The greatest. When I think of how I almost lost him it scares me." Emma had not only lied to Carrie and Sam about her family's wealth, she'd also lied to Kurt Ackerman.

Kurt was a handsome swimming instructor at the country club. Emma and he had begun dating and things were quickly getting serious. There was only one problem. Kurt was a townie whose family had lived on Sunset Island for years. His family was poor, which was why Kurt also drove a taxi some nights. Emma had been afraid to tell him about her family. She was afraid he'd think she was just another one of the spoiled rich kids he was always joking about. Then, when the truth came out, Kurt had been furious that she'd lied to him. It was only three nights ago that they'd made up. Now Emma was back on cloud nine.

The girls went out the side stage door, which opened into a parking lot. A beat-up sedan was parked right outside the door. Sitting on the hood, his back against the windshield, was Kurt. His lean, muscular arms rested comfortably behind his head and he seemed lost in a different world as he gazed up at the canopy of stars.

Quietly, Emma crept up to the car. Then, with the lithe grace of a cat, she lunged at him, tickling his ribs. "Aaah!" he cried out, but in seconds he'd gotten hold of both her wrists. "Now what?" he teased. "Now what are you going to do?"

"Hmmmmmm? This!" said Emma, leaning forward to kiss him. Kurt let go of her wrists and wrapped her in his arms. They kissed slowly and passionately.

"Aren't they cute together?" sighed Sam. "A little too cute, maybe. But cute nonetheless."

"Can you imagine what their kids would look like?" suggested Carrie. "They both have the most gorgeous blue eyes, great bods, and perfect teeth. Their kids couldn't go wrong."

"And they're both nice, too," Sam added. "It *is* slightly sickening, if you stop to think about it."

Emma and Kurt finally broke off their long embrace. They both looked a little dazed, as though they'd just lost track of where they were.

"Hi, remember us?" Sam said, seizing the moment. "As much as I hate to interrupt you two mammals during mating season, you did promise me a ride home. Carrie, too."

"Sorry," Kurt laughed, running a tanned hand through his sun-streaked light brown hair. "Hop in."

The girls were opening the doors when Sam spotted Lorell Courtland, Diana De Witt, and Daphne Whittinger coming toward them. "Oh, no! It's the three-headed she-monster from hell," Sam hissed. "Quick, run for your lives."

But Lorell and her friends were already upon them. "Why, look at this. Will wonders never cease!" crooned Lorell in a singsong Southern accent. She was a slim girl with sleek black hair and a deep tan, but her self-infatuated expression nearly ruined her good looks. The irritating timbre of her voice was another big minus. "Kurt, I see you forgave little ol' Emma for lyin' about being fabulously wealthy. Now isn't that sweet of you?"

The girls had met Lorell at the au pair convention. Lorell was only there under duress from her wealthy father, who thought a summer job would build his daughter's character. Lorell had had mixed feelings when no one hired her. On the one hand, she was delighted to escape the prospect of work. On the other, she was slightly mystified at having so underwhelmed her potential employers.

But, to the dismay of Sam, Emma, and Carrie, who'd all found her pretentious snobbishness completely disgusting, Lorell had ended up on Sunset Island after all. Her father had prevailed, finding her a job with his friends, the Popes.

"Wait until I tell our old classmates from Aubergame that our own Emma found herself a boy toy and went slumming this summer," purred Diana. Like Emma, Diana had just graduated from Aubergame, an exclusive Swiss girls' boarding school, but she and Emma were not friends. Far from it. They loathed each other. Diana's jealousy of everything about Emma manifested itself in brazen obnoxiousness.

Thin, nervous Daphne said nothing, but just stood there looking smug. She was a slight blond girl who looked as if a strong wind might blow her away. Her rich family owned a house on the island and Diana was her houseguest.

"Haven't you heard?" Kurt said coolly. "Emma's been disowned. She and I just bought a sailboat with the money I was saving for college. At the end of the summer we plan to sail around the world. We'll be poor, but who cares when you're passionately, madly in love? I mean madly, madly, *madly* in love."

The wildness in Kurt's eyes made the three girls back up. "I do believe you are mad. Both of you," Lorell said shrilly as the three girls scurried away.

"Oooooh baby!" laughed Sam. "Wait till that story gets around the island."

Emma was staring, wide-eyed, at Kurt. "Where did all that come from?"

"They're going to gossip, so why not give them something interesting to talk about?" he replied. "I think it's a pretty good story."

"Mmmm. I liked it, too," said Emma, looking at Kurt meaningfully. "Especially the 'passionately, madly' part."

"Me, too," agreed Kurt, returning her glance.

Carrie ahem-ed loudly. "I'm sorry to be a pain, but Ian and the babysitter have probably eloped by now. I really have to get home."

They piled into the car and Kurt started the engine. As they pulled out of the parking lot, Carrie caught sight of Flirting with Danger's van. She saw Billy sliding the side door of the van shut. He noticed her and waved. Then he opened the door to the driver's seat. Carrie sucked in her breath sharply. Sitting up front, squeezed into the passenger seat beside Pres, was Kristy Powell.

Sam saw Kristy, too. "Are you going to just play dead and let her take your man?" she asked.

"He's not my man," scoffed Carrie.

"He could be," Sam told her seriously. "Your problem is that you'll never snag him if you don't loosen up a little."

Carrie was too interested in what Sam had to say to be offended. "What do you mean, exactly?" she asked, leaning back on the worn seat of Kurt's car.

"Jeez-Louise!" Sam exclaimed. She began counting off on her fingers. "First of all, you could wear more makeup. You could also let some of your curves show. You're, like, not showing yourself to best advantage. Why hide what you've got?"

"I don't have a great figure," Carrie disagreed.

"And you're too modest," Sam said. "I'm not saying you should be a walking ego like that bitch Kristy. But it's okay to admit the truth. And the truth is, you're stacked!"

"Sam!" Carrie said, relieved the darkness hid her blush.

"You're curvy. That drives guys crazy. They love curvy." Sam was not known for her tact and restraint.

"Leave Carrie alone," Emma said. "You're embarrassing her."

"No, I'm not," Sam protested. "Besides, the girl needs to be told."

Kurt kept quiet as they turned up the hill towards posh Thorn Hill Road, where the Templetons lived.

"Well, you're embarrassing me," said Emma. "I think Carrie looks fine the way she is. Maybe a little makeup wouldn't hurt. But otherwise, she's fine."

"How can you say that?" Sam practically yelled at Emma. "You wear short shorts, and you're wearing a mini tonight. You don't keep yourself all covered up. I'm just saying a little cleavage wouldn't hurt. Carrie's my friend. I'm trying to help her."

"I don't *want* to look like Kristy," Carrie reminded Sam.

"Well, I'm not saying to hang your boobs out," Sam huffed.

"Sam!" Emma and Carrie shouted at the same time.

"Sorry, Kurt," Sam said breezily. "Facts are facts."

"It's okay," Kurt told her, laughing. "I can handle it."

"Well, *I* can't," Carrie said. "Sam, will you *please* shut up? I love you and I'm still your friend, but enough already!"

"No guts, no glory," Sam muttered rebelliously. "Remember that."

Kurt pulled up to a small toll house and rolled down the window. A guard waved a small flashlight around the car. He was one of the private security guards who watched over the five mansions up on Thorn Hill. "Hi, Harry," said Kurt. "I'm taking Carrie up to the Templetons'."

"Okay," said Harry, shutting off his flashlight.

"That must be the easiest job on earth," said Sam. "It's not like there's a big crime problem on this island. Who are they protecting these houses from?"

"Fans and fruitcakes, mostly," said Kurt, continuing up the moonlit road. "You don't have much crime here because of the ferry. They can stake out anybody trying to leave the island who might look suspicious. If they really have to, they can stop the ferries completely until they find the person they're looking for. That way the crook is trapped on the island. Besides, everyone around here knows one another. You can't hide much in this place."

"You mentioned fruitcakes," said Sam. "That sounds intriguing."

"Well, you have to figure, you have Graham Templeton, Helena Ross, Mrs. G., Ronald Crumpster, and Sheena Morley all on this one hill," he said, naming two rock stars, two society billionaires, and the supermodel ex-wife of a world-class prizefighter. "There are lots of flaky people who want to get in to see them. They do weird stuff like steal personal items, or they want autographs, or they just want to look at them."

"Has anyone ever done anything violent?" asked Carrie.

"No," Kurt assured her. "They got this private security force three years ago after some weirdo got into the Crumpsters' house and taped plans for a condominium community that he wanted to build all over the walls. He wanted Crumpster to back him. I think Sheena Morley wants to make sure her ex-husband doesn't show up, too. They used to have some bad fights. There's nothing to worry about, though."

"Good," said Carrie. "I guess we are kind of isolated up here. It's nice having the security guards."

Kurt pulled up in front of the huge glass-and-white-stucco mansion. "Why does anyone need a house this big?" he wondered aloud.

"Claudia says they like to entertain," said Carrie, stepping out of the car. "So far, I haven't seen them do anything but go out."

Carrie noticed Emma looking blankly out the window. Obviously she didn't want to get into a conversation about why the rich did the things they did. Carrie wished Emma didn't feel that way, because she'd have liked to ask her some questions about how really rich people saw the world.

This summer Carrie often recalled a line written by F. Scott Fitzgerald: "The rich are different from you and me." Before coming to Sunset Island, Carrie had thought the line ridiculous. Of course all people were the same. Her own family was upper-middle-class. They bought nice clothes, ate in nice restaurants, and took nice vacations. They were like anyone else.

Now Carrie realized that Fitzgerald wasn't

talking about people like her family, with their expensive foreign cars and frequent-flyer bonuses. He was talking about the super-rich. The megarich. And even if they weren't essentially different at heart, the lives they lived—they way they thought, what they expected from life, how they perceived themselves—certainly were different. Their lives were easier; they expected more, and usually got it. They took for granted the luxuries that other people worked a lifetime for but often never attained. They *were* different.

"See you tomorrow," Sam called as Carrie stepped out of the car and headed for the door. "Thanks again for the passes."

"Yes, thanks a lot," echoed Emma, waving out the window while Kurt turned the car around in the wide, elegant white-gravel driveway.

Using her key, Carrie let herself in the front door. "Carrie! Carrie! Carrie!" Four-year-old Chloe came tottering toward Carrie wearing a pair of large high heels, her arms stretched wide. Behind her trailed one of her mother's expensive gauzy gowns, which Chloe loved to wear. Her large brown eyes were bright with excitement. And, as usual, her uncombed auburn curls rose around her head like a fuzzy halo.

"Hi, sweet pea," said Carrie, stooping to give her a hug. "Why aren't you asleep?"

"I was waiting for you," replied Chloe, laying her head on Carrie's shoulder.

"Did your mom say you could wear those things?" Carrie asked.

"Uh-uh," Chloe admitted truthfully. "But they were just laying on the floor in her room. She won't mind."

"Well, let's take them off you. I think your mom would mind. Didn't she give you some *old* things for dress-up?"

"Her new things are prettier," Chloe argued mildly.

"I know." Carrie smiled. "That's why she doesn't want you to play with them." Putting Chloe down, she lifted the dress over her head. It probably had cost a fortune, yet Claudia had casually tossed it aside in her bedroom. "We'll just throw this in Mom's room and she won't know you had it on," said Carrie, resisting the urge to fold the dress neatly. That would have been a dead giveaway that Chloe had been wearing it.

After tossing the dress and shoes into the master bedroom, Carrie picked Chloe up and walked down the stairs to the glassed-in living room with its spectacular ocean view. She'd expected to find Ian and the babysitter watching the wide-screen TV in there, but they weren't anywhere in sight. Carrie looked in the open country-style kitchen, which stood on a platform overlooking the living room. No one was there, either. "Where is Ian?" Carrie asked Chloe.

"He's swimming with the babysitter. Her name is Brenda," said Chloe.

"What?" shrieked Carrie. "Where?"

"Down-tairs," she said. Chloe had trouble with

syllables that began with *s*, so *stairs* became *tairs*.

With Chloe still in her arms, Carrie hurried down a set of plush carpeted stairs that led to the Olympic-sized indoor pool in the basement. On the diving board stood Brenda the babysitter, a tall, thin blonde, wearing nothing but an oversized T-shirt and her underpants. "Watch this one, Ian baby," she said happily, bouncing on the board. "A super cannonball." Her young voice had a hollow, echoey ring in the high-ceilinged, tiled room.

Under the diving board treading water was twelve-year-old Ian. Carrie was relieved to see he was at least wearing a bathing suit. He was Graham's son from his first marriage. Graham's first wife and Ian's mother, Sirena, had died when Ian was two. The rumor was that she'd overdosed on drugs, though Carrie had never witnessed Graham even taking a drink.

"Ready, set—" called Brenda. When she saw Carrie coming toward her, she stopped bouncing. Carrie couldn't help but notice that her small, braless breasts kept bouncing a while longer. Carrie glanced quickly at Ian and saw that his eyes were riveted to the same spot. "Hi there," Brenda said, waving at Carrie with an unconcerned smile.

Carrie didn't smile back. "Why was Chloe running around upstairs by herself?" Carrie demanded angrily.

"Hey, relax. I thought she was asleep," said the

girl, climbing down from the board and wrapping herself in a towel. "She zonked out on the couch watching some videos."

"And you didn't put her in bed," said Carrie flatly.

"Why? She looked comfortable," Brenda replied, an annoyed edge coming into her voice.

"And what are you doing swimming down here?" Carrie asked. "Do you have your lifeguard certification? If Ian had a cramp or something, could you have saved him?"

"Chill out, would you?" said Brenda. "The kid can swim fine. He's not going to drown, Carrie baby."

Carrie felt like slapping the girl. She was completely irresponsible and then had the nerve to be insolent and defensive about it. "I think you'd better go upstairs and get dressed," Carrie said with suppressed fury.

Brenda glared at her and walked away, dripping onto the cement floor. "Bitch," Carrie heard her mutter loudly under her breath.

It took every ounce of self-control Carrie possessed to keep from tossing the girl into the pool. She looked over at Ian, who was gazing back at her sheepishly. At twelve, he had more sense then thirteen-year-old Brenda. *At least he knows he's done something wrong*, thought Carrie.

Ian perched on the side of the pool. His short, spiky blond hair glistened with water. The blond tail that had been left long in the back dripped water down his thin shoulder. "Are you mad?" he asked.

"Not at you," said Carrie, setting Chloe down and squatting down to talk to Ian. "Not really. I mean, Brenda was supposed to be in charge. But, Ian, you know you're not allowed down here without an adult."

"I was with Brenda," said Ian.

Carrie sighed. Technically, he did have a point. Brenda was the adult authority figure for the night—as laughable as that was. "Come on," said Carrie, extending her hand to Ian. "You're supposed to be in bed."

Ian scrambled out of the pool and Carrie handed him a towel. He was a handsome boy, but small for his age. He'd just turned twelve in June and was very anxious to start growing. Claudia had told him that boys often shoot up in one summer. That had made Ian hopeful that this would be his summer. His dearest wish was that when he began seventh grade in the fall he would no longer be the shortest kid in his class.

Upstairs, Brenda was waiting for her father to come pick her up. She was wearing a pink mini with a matching halter top, which was cut short at the midriff. Carrie paid her quickly. "I'll wait for my father outside," said Brenda. She turned to Ian. "So long, Ian baby. It was fun."

Again, Carrie noticed Ian's eyes light up like a puppy who had just been offered a bone. "Bye, Brenda," he said, following her every move as she walked toward the door.

Chloe yawned and yanked Carrie's hand. "I'm tired."

Lifting Chloe, Carrie watched Brenda shut the door behind her. *This is just great, she thought dismally. There goes a thirteen-year-old girl who's hotter and sexier than I am.*

Maybe it is *time to do something with my image, after all.*

THREE

"Hi, guys!" Carrie called as she made her way across the crowded porch of the Play Café. Sam and Emma were seated at a small table on the open deck of the popular hangout. Carrie hadn't seen them since the concert two nights earlier. But finally, late Monday afternoon, their three schedules had coincided, giving them time off together.

"Howdy, stranger," Sam said as Carrie tucked her oversized beachbag under a chair. "You look tired and hungry and thirsty. But you're in luck. We already ordered for you."

"Thanks," said Carrie, taking a seat. The Play Café was known for its live rock music on the weekends, its great burgers, and its terrible service. "I *am* kind of tired," Carrie added. "I was with Ian and Chloe at the beach all day yesterday, then I sat for them at night, and I took them to the beach again today. Finally Claudia picked them up from the beach because someone invited the family to a barbecue."

"I can't believe we haven't seen each other for

two days," said Emma. "Is it my imagination, or is the summer getting busier and busier?"

"It's definitely getting busier," said Carrie, twisting her hair back and fastening it with a clip. "Every time you turn around the town is sponsoring some outdoor concert or tournament or show. Which is great, but not great, if you know what I mean."

"I do know what you mean," said Sam. "It's great for the kids, but not for us. It very seriously interferes with my side jobs."

"What side jobs are those?" Emma asked, raising a suspicious eyebrow.

"Partying and patrolling the beach for guys!" Sam answered, as though the answer should have been obvious.

"Oh, of course! Why didn't I realize?" laughed Emma.

"Get with it, girl," Sam joked. She turned to Carrie. "The monsters told me you were a real *b-i-t-c-h* to their little friend Brenda the other night. Good for you. I hate that kid. She's always over at the house."

Carrie told her friends about the state of affairs she'd encountered when she returned to the Templetons' house. "Thirteen is such a weird age," she added. "For some kids it's old enough to babysit. My thirteen-year-old sister babysits and she does a great job. She's so mature and responsible. But other thirteen-year-olds—like Allie and Becky—still need a babysitter themselves."

"Allie and Becky need a zookeeper," quipped Sam.

Just then a young, harried-looking waitress named Patsi arrived at their table with a tray of food. "Three burger deluxes with everything. Three chocolate shakes. And one Death by Chocolate cake with three forks," she said, reading off their order as she hurriedly placed it on the table.

"Why didn't you just order a tub of lard so I could apply it directly to my hips?" moaned Carrie.

"Sam ordered before I got here," said Emma, who was by nature a light eater.

"Come on, you two, you only live once," said Sam, biting into her burger.

"Sure." Carrie laughed ironically as she picked up a fry. "If I have only one life to live, let me live it as a gigantic blimp. Why not?"

"Hey, you should thank me for ordering only one piece of cake," Sam defended herself.

Suddenly Emma tapped Carrie's arm excitedly. "Look, Billy Sampson just got here. He's over there."

Carrie spotted Billy coming up the porch steps. He wore jeans and a neon-green sleeveless T-shirt. His cheekbones were highlighted by a touch of new, pink sunburn. "God, he's gorgeous," sighed Carrie, swooning back in her chair.

"You are a dim and hopeless child," chided Sam. "Sit up straight and get with the program." Immediately Sam began waving her hand over her head. "Yo, Billy!"

Billy's face lit up when he spotted the girls. "Hello, ladies," he called, returning Sam's greeting as he headed toward them. Almost instinctively, Carrie sat up straight in her seat.

"Lose the shirt," Sam muttered between clenched teeth, referring to the frayed green camp shirt Carrie had thrown over her blue tank suit.

"I can't just take it off," Carrie muttered back. "That's too obvious."

Just as Billy was almost at their table, Sam swung her hand out, splattering a milkshake all over Carrie's shirt. "Oh, I am *so* sorry!" Sam apologized insincerely.

Carrie jumped to her feet. "Sam!" she cried, but in the next second she realized Sam had done it on purpose. It was all she could do not to burst into laughter, even though she was also kind of annoyed. "I guess I'd better take this shirt off," she said.

"Yes, I guess you'd better," Sam agreed sweetly.

"A little accident there, huh?" noted Billy, pulling a chair up to the table and sitting on it backwards.

"I am so clumsy sometimes," said Sam. "I don't know what to do with myself."

Carrie undid her shirt and stuffed it into her beachbag. All around her girls sat confidently in shorts and bikini tops. What was wrong with her? Why was she so nervous about being seen in a tank suit? She wished she weren't so modest, but she couldn't help it. She'd always been that way.

"How was the party?" she asked Billy.

"Fun. Too bad you couldn't make it," he said. "Graham and Claudia even came by for a little while. Listen to this: A friend of theirs who owns a recording studio over in Portland came to the concert. His name is Sid Klein. He likes our sound, but he says that our demo is too amateurish. He's going to let us use his studio to record another. He's doing it as a favor to Graham. And get this: Graham says he'll listen to the new demo. If it's any good, he'll talk to the execs at his record company for us."

"Graham is very generous and he could really help you a lot," Carrie observed.

"You're telling me. One session in a first-rate recording studio can cost a mint. Our last tape was done in a studio, but not a first-rate one. We knew the sound could have been better but it was the best we could do at the time. This will be a giant difference."

"I thought your tape sounded great," Carrie said loyally. She meant it, too. It was true Howie had a terrific sound system, but that could only do so much. She'd really been impressed with the music when Howie played the tape.

"Yeah, well, I hope you'll think it sounds even greater when you hear the next one," Billy told her. "This could be a big break for us. Maybe even bigger than Graham letting us open for him Saturday."

"That's fantastic," said Emma. "Sounds as if you're really on your way to the big time."

"I'm keeping my fingers crossed," Billy said. He looked around the restaurant. "I'm starving. Has anyone seen Patsi?"

"She's come and gone," Sam told him. "You know her—once she's delivered your food, you might not see her again for hours, months, years even."

"That's the truth," Billy agreed. "I'd better go find her." As he got up he added, "You guys don't mind if I join you, do you?"

The three girls spoke at once.

"Of course not!"

"Nope!"

"Uh-uh."

Billy smiled. "Thanks. I'll be right back."

Sam jabbed Carrie's shoulder excitedly as soon as he'd gone. "See, I told you he likes you," she whispered. "Did you see the way he was looking at you?"

"I'm a mess," Carrie groaned, feeling stupid with her hair pulled back. Still, inside she was fluttering with excitement. He *had* been looking at her more than at Emma and Sam. She casually reached up and unclipped her hair.

Sam dumped the contents of a small cosmetics bag onto the table. "Go to the ladies' room while he's gone and spruce up. Let's see, what do you need? Here's mascara, some lipstick, and some purple eyeshadow."

"I can't. He'll notice," Carrie protested. "Besides, I never use that stuff. I'll never get it on right."

"Well, brush your hair at least!" cried Sam, frustrated.

Emma dug into the pocket of her baggy floral-print shorts. "Here," she said, laying three small makeup cylinders on the table. "This is just clear lip gloss, translucent blush gel, and clear mascara. It just glistens up your lashes. It's my beach makeup. It won't be too noticeable."

"Okay, I'll give it a try," Carrie said. It seemed the easiest way out. After all, the last thing she wanted was for Sam to make a scene.

She couldn't entirely avoid it, though. Sam took a small bottle of spray cologne from her cosmetics bag and began squirting Carrie. "Get out of here," Carrie said, waving Sam away. "It stinks."

"It does not stink. It's alluring!" Sam corrected her. "It says so right on the label."

"Well, keep it off me, okay?" Carrie said lightly, getting up.

As Carrie made her way to the bathroom inside the restaurant, she was aware of several boys at different tables checking her out. She didn't know them and wasn't interested, but still, it gave her a pleasant thrill to be . . . what was the word? Admired? Lusted after? *Oh, maybe they're looking because they can't believe how much I reek of cheap perfume*, she scolded herself. *Don't get such big ideas, girl.*

Carrie crossed the cool, shadowy dance area

where bands played on weekends. Rays of soft, late-afternoon light cut across the floor from the windows. The room was an oasis of calm and quiet compared to the bustle on the porch and in the indoor dining-and-pool-room area next door.

At the far end of the dance floor was one of the rest rooms. Carrie had discovered that on weekdays that bathroom was usually empty even when there was a line for the ladies' room in the dining area.

In the dingy, badly lit bathroom, Carrie put on Emma's makeup. She did look nice. Herself, but better somehow. She almost sparkled. Then she bent forward and brushed out her hair until it shone.

Not wanting to be gone too long, Carrie stuffed the makeup into the pockets of her jean shorts and left the bathroom. Crossing the dance floor, she stopped just before stepping onto the porch. Two thin mirrored panels flanked the doorway. Carrie inspected her image one last time.

The sight she saw made her stop short. Responding to the chill of the bathroom, her nipples had gotten hard. They stood up clearly and firmly beneath the nylon of her suit. *Don't be such a prude,* she scolded herself. Another girl might not have given it a second thought, but Carrie's innate modesty stopped her from going outside like that. *What do I do now?* she wondered.

She didn't have time to worry about it for long.

"There you are," said Billy, stepping into the room.

"Oh, hi," said Carrie, flustered.

"Listen, I wanted to talk to you alone." He leaned up against the wall. His eyes swept over her, lingering for less than a split second on her breasts, then moving up to her eyes. Once again, his gaze was like a strong hand running up the length of her body. It kindled a warm glow deep inside her.

"Would you like to come to a party at the recording studio in Portland? This Sid character is throwing it and he invited the band," he told her. "I couldn't ask everybody since it's not our party, but it would be great if you could come."

"It sounds like fun," she answered, trying to keep her voice level. "I've never been to a recording studio. When's the party?"

"Tomorrow night."

Tomorrow night! No! Carrie was supposed to sit for Ian and Chloe the next evening. But she couldn't tell him that. It would be the second time in two days she'd turned him down. He'd think she wasn't interested. Maybe Emma or Sam could sit for her. Graham and Claudia might not mind that. "Sure, I can go," she said.

"Cool," he replied, smiling. "I'll pick you up around nine."

"No," she said quickly. "I'll meet you at the ferry. Graham and Claudia are funny about people coming to the house."

"Okay," he agreed. "We can take the nine-thirty ferry to Portland. I'll meet you at the ticket house."

"Terrific," she said. At that moment Patsi passed by outside the door.

"Excuse me," said Billy. "I'm still trying to catch her. Do you want anything? Another milk-shake?"

"Uh, no, that's okay. I mean, thanks." Carrie felt like she was babbling. She was so nervous!

"You sure?" Billy smiled at her and her heart did a little flip. "It's no trouble . . . maybe a Coke or something?"

"A Coke would be great," Carrie told him. "Thanks."

"I'll see you back at the table," Billy said, launching himself after Patsi. Then he paused and turned back for a moment. "By the way, you look dynamite in that suit," he told her.

Carrie smiled. "Thanks."

"Yes!" she whispered triumphantly when he'd gone. "Yes! Yes! Yes!" He *did* like her. More than like her. He was attracted to her. Maybe he'd realized it for the first time just now. The hair, the makeup . . . her breasts. It had all worked in her favor. He was turned on. There was no doubt about it. It was written all over his handsome face.

Tossing back her hair and squaring her shoulders, she walked out onto the porch. "What happened to you?" asked Sam when she returned to the table. She and Emma had finished their burgers and were starting on the chocolate cake.

Carrie leaned forward excitedly. "He asked me out."

"That's wonderful. Where? When?" asked Emma.

"To a party at a recording studio in Portland tomorrow night," Carrie breathed blissfully.

"Oh, totally cool," crooned Sam.

"There's just one problem," Carrie began. "I'm supposed to—"

Carrie was interrupted by Billy's return. "I'm going to have to skip the burger. It'll take too long and I really can't be late for band practice, because Pres has to cut out early. So long, ladies." He cast Carrie a special, warm look. "See you tomorrow."

"See you," she replied.

"So, what's this problem?" Sam whispered anxiously as Billy walked away.

"The problem is that I have to take care of Ian and Chloe tomorrow night."

"Why don't they give it a break?" Sam cried, throwing her hands up in disgust. "Don't those two ever stay home? Why did they even bother having kids?"

Carrie felt guilty. She liked the Templetons, even if they were—in all innocence—ruining her love life. "They love the kids. They just like to go out a lot. That's how I came to have this great summer job." She sighed. "Anyway, I was thinking that maybe one of you could sit for them. Claudia and Graham know you. I don't think they'd mind. I'd pay you," she added.

"Oh, Carrie, you wouldn't have to pay me. I'd

do anything for you. But I can't do this," Sam said. "The monsters are having a party and their poor, dear dad has a date." The twins lived with their divorced father. "I swore up and down that I'd be available tomorrow night."

"What about you, Emma?" Carrie asked.

Emma's rueful expression made Carrie's heart sink.

"You have a date with Kurt," Carrie surmised.

"Oh, no. I'd break a date if it were that. Kurt would understand. No, Jeff and Jane are entertaining a big client tomorrow night. It could mean millions of dollars for their law firm," Emma explained. "They need to have the kids completely out of their hair. They want me to feed them, bathe them, and get them to bed without a peep."

Folding her arms on the table, Carrie dropped her head onto them. "I want to die," she mumbled.

"Come on." Sam tried to comfort her. "We'll think of something. What about getting that twerp Brenda back?"

Carrie lifted her head. "No way. She was awful, and anyway I told Graham and Claudia that she was too immature to sit again. Besides, she's probably going to the party at your house."

"That's true. What else can we do?" Sam mused.

"It's a shame that Ian isn't just a little older," said Emma. "He's almost old enough not to need a sitter at all."

"I know," Carrie agreed. "And once the kids are asleep, it's just a big waste of time. I mean, Chloe woke up the other night because she was on the couch. When she's in her bed and tucked in she doesn't ever wake up. Ian either. They both sleep like logs."

"Do you think Ian could handle an emergency?" asked Sam.

"Probably," said Carrie. "He's pretty mature for his age. Besides, those security guards are always just minutes away. Their beeper number is taped on all the phones. Why?"

"Who would really know if you just ducked out for a little while?" suggested Sam.

"I couldn't do that," said Carrie, aghast at the idea. "That would be . . . awful. Oh, I just couldn't."

Emma furrowed her brow thoughtfully. "I don't know. Ian *is* almost old enough to babysit. And the island is completely safe. Especially where you are, with the special security. But I know how you feel. The idea makes me uneasy, too."

"No. No way. I can't go out and leave them," Carrie said firmly.

At that moment Patsi arrived with Carrie's Coke. "Billy paid me for this already," she said as she set it down. "Anybody want anything else?"

"No thanks," said Carrie, poking her cold fries with her fork. "I think I've lost my appetite—forever."

"Well, that's one way to diet," said Patsi, clearing the dishes. "What's the bummer?"

"She had a date with Billy but she can't go because she has to sit," Emma said, filling her in. "Do you think a twelve-year-old is old enough to take care of himself and a four-year-old?"

"On this island, yeah," said Patsi confidently. "I was taking care of my five brothers when I was twelve, and I come from the South Side of Chicago."

"Waitress!" a guy called from his table across the porch.

"One minute," Patsi called back irritably. "Here is el checko, thank you very much, and I hope you solve your problem," she said, laying down the check. "By the way, how did you get Billy away from that ding-dong Kristy Powell? I thought she almost had him in the bag."

"She may have him yet," said Carrie glumly.

"Oh, well. Good luck," Patsi said as she went over to wait on the table that had summoned her.

The girls paid their check and left the Play Café. Carrie had the farthest distance to go. She walked her bike until Emma and Sam turned off. Then she hopped on and pedaled the rest of the way home. It was nearly six-thirty and the sunlight washed the shore road in gentle tones of gray-blue. She loved this time of day, the stillness of it. The only sound was the occasional cry of a seagull as it circled over the ocean in search of its supper.

The last leg of her journey, pedaling up Thorn

Hill, was the most difficult. Many of the wealthy people on the island had oceanfront property, but Claudia had told Carrie that she and Graham preferred the isolation and the spectacular view from atop Thorn Hill.

When she got to the house, the family was still out. Graham and Claudia liked to keep their household staff to a minimum during the summer. The cook, housekeeper, and driver all worked part-time during the day. That afternoon, gardeners had worked on the perfect lawn and brilliant flower garden, but they'd left by now. Carrie had the house all to herself.

She wandered through the open, airy rooms filled with expensive contemporary furniture and art objects collected from around the world. What a fabulous life these people had—so glamorous and fascinating.

Carrie compared Graham and Claudia's life to that of her parents. Her mother and father were both pediatricians, and the parents of five kids. Carrie was the oldest. They had money, but not on this scale. And they worked hard, very hard. Besides their regular practices, both of them put in a great amount of time at a clinic where they worked for almost nothing. Most nights they came home exhausted and burnt out. The idea of partying the way Graham and Claudia did would have been totally alien to them. In fact, her parents would probably consider Graham and Claudia's life frivolous.

And maybe it *was* frivolous, Carrie considered

as she climbed the stairs to her room. But it was exciting. Oh, so exciting. Her parents' earnest seriousness suddenly seemed like a dead weight dragging her down; the principles she'd been brought up with felt like a burden she could no longer bear. Be polite to everyone. Follow the rules, but stand up for what's right. Take responsibility for your actions. Say what you mean, but be diplomatic. Be honest. Work hard.

"Aaah!" Carrie cried out in a short burst of frustration. It all got to be too much sometimes. Why couldn't she—just once—throw off the burden of being Tom and Mary Beth Alden's responsible oldest daughter? *That's me, good old Carrie,* she thought. *Such a good student, so good with little kids, such a help around the house . . .*

So boring!

As she went down the upstairs hallway to her room, she passed Graham and Claudia's bedroom. The door was open and Carrie stopped to look in. It was lucky for them Mrs. Ball came in every other day and cleaned. This was an in-between day, and their room looked like both their closets had exploded.

Carrie stepped into the room. Claudia's expensive gypsy wardrobe was tossed everywhere. A flowered chiffon skirt was flung over their bed's brass headboard. High-heeled shoes and wedge-heel sandals looked as if they'd been kicked in the air and now lay where they'd landed on the plush white carpet. The two sandy pieces of Claudia's fringed bikini lay tangled in the middle of the floor.

Graham was no better. Sheet music, music industry magazines, and a man's silk robe were strewn on the unmade bed, across the elegant Oriental-design quilt.

This mess offended Carrie's orderly nature. Without thinking, she began picking up Claudia's shoes, putting them in a neat line under the bed. As she reached out for a gold sandal that had been kicked under the bed, hot tears suddenly began streaming down her cheeks.

Are you getting your period, dear? That's what her mother would have said if she'd walked in right then and seen her weeping over a line of shoes. But she wasn't getting her period. She was nowhere near her period. She was just fed up with being good and sweet and responsible.

She was tired of being the kind of person who went around tidying other people's shoes.

With a sweep of her arm she scattered the shoes across the room. Something was going to have to change. And that something was going to be Carrie Alden.

FOUR

"I can't look." Carrie cringed, covering her eyes.

Riiiipppppppppppp. Sam tore the side seam of the new neon-orange T-shirt dress Carrie wore, opening it up to the thigh. They were in Carrie's small, neat room. It was early evening on the night of Carrie's date.

Carrie had lain awake for a long time the night before, and had finally made a decision. She was going to the party and she was going to look hot. Sam was right: not only was it time for an image overhaul, it was also time to play with the big kids. No more girl next door!

Sam opened a plastic box full of large gold safety pins and began pinning them into the frayed seam, linking them together as she pinned. "I saw this in a magazine last week," she said. "I've been dying to try it." Soon the slit in the skirt was laced with pins. Sam stood back and pensively jiggled the pins remaining in the box. "It needs something else." Then her eyes brightened with an idea.

She picked up a small cuticle scissors from Carrie's dresser and cut right down the center of the scooped neckline. "That's low enough," Carrie cried. Sam blithely continued cutting down to a point not far above her navel.

"Don't stop me when I'm in the throes of creativity," she said. "I'm making fashion history here."

"Great," Carrie replied, rolling her eyes.

Starting at the bottom, Sam pinned the neckline back up to an inch below Carrie's collarbone. She stepped back to admire her work. "I'm a genius. The pins draw attention to your legs and your chest. Exactly where you want it. I think it needs a belt, though." Sam dug into her large canvas tote, which sat on the bed. "I just happen to have brought a selection of my very best belts."

Sam laid four belts on the bed. She picked out one that was made up of a series of hammered copper discs linked together with strips of black suede. In the center of each disc was set a pale amber stone. "The amber stones are perfect with the dress," she decided. "Which, by the way, is an awesome color with your hair and eyes."

"Thanks, but it'll never fit me," Carrie objected. "I don't like belts, anyway. My waist is too thick."

"You do not have a thick waist," Sam scoffed as she wrapped the belt around Carrie. "Oh, please. Look how perfect this is." Sam hooked the belt closed, then stepped back to study the effect. "Get rid of the bra."

"Absolutely not."

"This is supposed to be the new you!"

"Sam!"

"Car—rie," Sam mimicked her. "Will you please grow up? And lighten up. You'll *ruin* my creation if you don't take it off."

Carrie looked down forlornly at the telltale white line showing between the pins. "I *told* you to stop cutting," she reminded Sam.

"Yeah, well, I didn't," Sam said breezily. "Come on, a goody-goody like you can't possibly go out with your *underwear* showing."

Reluctantly, Carrie slid the T-shirt dress down her shoulders to take off her bra.

"Much better," Sam said, satisfied. "Now that wasn't too bad, was it?"

"Easy for you to say," Carrie muttered, but all the same she couldn't help smiling. Sam's recklessness and insouciance *were* a little catching.

"Maybe by next week we can get you to leave out the underwear entirely," Sam teased. "Just kidding," she added quickly, seeing Carrie's shocked expression.

Picking up a thick brush, Sam swept Carrie's hair up into a ponytail on the top of her head. Then she deftly loosened a few strands of hair so that the wispy pieces fringed Carrie's face. "*Très* fetching," Sam said, admiring her handiwork.

Just then Claudia called from downstairs. "We're leaving, Carrie."

"Quick, my robe!" cried Carrie.

Sam held up Carrie's cornflower-blue terry robe and Carrie scurried into it. She ran down the hall in her bare feet, tying the robe tightly around her.

Claudia stood at the bottom of the stairs looking stunning in a sheer red flowered skirt over lacy black capri leggings, topped with an off-the-shoulder black blouse. Her hair was pulled back in a French braid, exposing long silver-beaded earrings. A fringed black brocade shawl was draped casually around her arms.

"We'll be hopping all over tonight," she told Carrie, who had perched on an upper step. "I left phone numbers tacked to the refrigerator. The kids are watching *The Little Mermaid*. It was Chloe's turn to pick a video."

"Okay, I was just getting changed. I'll be right down," said Carrie. Her voice was calm, but her heart was racing. How could she do this to Claudia? The woman trusted her completely. She couldn't possibly sneak out tonight. Not in a million years.

Graham came into the hallway looking every inch a rock star with his slicked-back hair and his perfectly tailored yet effortlessly casual linen summer suit. "Cute hair," he said, noting Carrie's new hairdo.

"Yes, I was just about to say so, too," Claudia agreed. "It looks terrific that way!"

"I decided to try something different," Carrie explained quickly, irrationally fearing they'd somehow suspect something was out of the ordinary.

"I don't know when we'll be home, so just lock up before you go to sleep," Graham said as he held open the front door for Claudia.

"Sure thing," Carrie said. "Have fun."

The minute the door shut, Carrie leapt up and charged back to her room. "I can't do it," she told Sam. "It's not right. I would be letting Claudia and Graham down."

"I've been thinking about it, too," said Sam. "Let me ask you a question. How did Claudia meet Graham?"

"What?" Carrie said.

"Trust me, it's relevant," Sam insisted. "How?"

"Well, she was working as a secretary, for Mr. Rudolph, I think. Then, after Sirena died, Graham started relying on her more and more to help him with Ian and personal stuff like making travel arrangements and all. Pretty soon she started traveling with him as his personal secretary, and then they fell in love and got married."

"Just like that, huh?" said Sam skeptically.

"That's the story. But what does that have to do with anything?"

"You can be really naive, Carrie," sighed Sam. "A little twenty-one-year-old secretary doesn't land a rock legend without putting all her mind and all her energy to it. You can bet Claudia didn't let anyone or anything stop her when it came to getting Graham. And look at her now.

She's got a roomful of shoes and she's Mr. Rudolph's boss!"

"What's your point?" asked Carrie.

"My point is that if Claudia were you, she would do exactly what you're doing tonight. She wouldn't hang back and say, 'Oh, I just couldn't.'"

"Well, in the first place I don't think that's true. Graham and Claudia have a really good relationship and I know she adores him. I just don't believe she set out to *get him*, as you so romantically put it. You make it sound like she ambushed him."

Sam rolled her eyes.

"And anyway," Carrie went on, "even if that is true, I don't want to be that way, Sam! I'm not trying to snag Billy. I'm not trying to trick him into liking me or something!"

Sam folded her arms. "Then why were you so hell-bent on sneaking out just ten minutes ago?"

"Weeell . . . I'm just afraid that if I turn him down twice in a row—even if it *is* true that I have to babysit—he'll think I'm just making lame excuses to avoid going out with him. He'll think I don't like him. And I do!" she finished passionately.

"Exactly," Sam said. "You are simply letting him know that the attraction is mutual. What could be more honest than that?"

Sam was so persuasive. And she certainly seemed to know what she was talking about when it came to guys. Carrie wavered. It was true: ten minutes before, she'd thought it was a great idea. Why was she suddenly having second thoughts? The old Carrie, the responsible do-right girl next door, was hard to banish in favor of the new, carefree version who dressed like a vamp and broke rules.

"Do you think so? Oh, maybe you're right," Carrie said finally. "What do I know? It's true. All my life I've always been such a goody-goody."

"Of course I'm right," Sam said. "Now, quick, let me do your makeup. I have to be home by seven to supervise this living nightmare of twenty teenyboppers who are about to destroy the Jacobses' home. I can't believe Mr. Jacobs expects me, alone, to save his house from complete and total annihilation by a nymphette party."

Carrie laughed as she pulled a straight-backed chair in front of her full-length mirror. "If anyone can keep the beasts in line, it's you," she said.

Sam knelt at her side and began to apply eyeshadow in layers of purple, lavender, and rose. She lined Carrie's eyes with a purple pencil and smudged it carefully. "Time to make those lips stand up and scream 'kiss me!'" she said, sharpening a lip pencil over the trash basket. "You'd look great with collagen injections to give you that pouty, bee-stung look guys love."

"Nobody's sticking needles in my lips," said Carrie. "No way! All this cosmetic surgery stuff is too weird, if you ask me."

"I'd get it if I could afford it," said Sam,

carefully lining Carrie's lips so that they appeared wider and fuller. "All the models are getting it done. I saw a talk show where a model said you just can't compete unless you have fat lips."

"Are you still thinking about modeling?" asked Carrie when Sam stopped lining.

"Since I got here, everyone's been telling me I should be a model, so maybe I should be," she said, carefully covering Carrie's lips with a bright, deep red color. "I was talking to Flash on the beach the other day and—"

"Who?" Carrie interrupted.

"Don't move your lips," Sam scolded. "Flash Hathaway. You remember that guy we met at Howie's party. The one who's a photographer for Universal Models."

"That slimeball?" cried Carrie.

"Don't talk while I'm making lips," Sam said. "He is a little slimy, I'll admit. But I can handle him. And he's here scouting for new talent. He says I've got what it takes. He wants me to meet him for a drink to talk about it some more."

Sam had stopped working. "Can I talk now?" Carrie asked.

"Just until I find my lip gloss," Sam replied, kneeling down to dig through her makeup case.

"What about your dance scholarship to Kansas State?"

"I'm a pretty good dancer," replied Sam, sitting back on her heels. "But dancing is something I do for fun. It's not my passion or anything. I took the scholarship because it was the one I got. I also applied for an academic scholarship, an art scholarship, and a scholarship sponsored by the Elks Club. It didn't mean I wanted to be an Elk."

Sam wrinkled her nose. "Gosh, do you think I'd have had to become an Elk if I'd gotten it? Are there girl Elks? Elkettes? Maybe it's a good thing I didn't get that scholarship. I'd hate to have to wear one of those weird hats with horns, like Fred Flintstone used to wear. On the other hand, maybe it would look kind of—"

"You were saying about the scholarship?" Carrie interrupted.

"Oh, yeah," said Sam, kneeling forward and putting on Carrie's lip gloss. "What I'm saying is that I needed a scholarship or I wasn't going to college. And in my town, if you don't go to college then you take some nowhere job in the front office of a pig slaughterhouse or something. You work there till you get so bored that the local jokers start looking good to you. Eventually your mind goes completely numb and you wind up marrying one of them."

"It sounds horrible," said Carrie.

"It is horrible. Though the idea doesn't bother a lot of the girls I went to high school with. Some of them are married already."

"Really?" asked Carrie. The thought of being married at eighteen was unbelievable to her.

"*Married with Children.* The whole scene. I guess they wanted to skip the working-the-jerky-job part and get right to it. So you can see why I was out-of-my-mind desperate to get to college. But now I have a possible third choice. And it sounds pretty good to me."

"Are you sure?" Carrie asked. "It wouldn't appeal to me at all. Doesn't it sound boring to stand around all day posing for pictures?"

"Oh, yeah, it sounds real boring," Sam said sarcastically. "I would hate to wear designer clothes, be paid gobs of money, travel all over the world, and hobnob with the rich and famous. You're right, it sounds like a total drag."

"I see your point," Carrie conceded.

Sam checked her watch. "Shoot! I've got to fly!" She grabbed her bag and headed for the door. "You look super. Now don't chicken out and change or anything."

"I won't," Carrie assured her. "Thanks. Oh, and remember what we talked about. I'm leaving your number on the fridge. If Ian should call you, you call me at the studio."

"Sid's Soundorama, right?"

"Right."

"Tacky name," Sam commented. "Don't worry. Everything will be fine."

When Sam was gone, Carrie looked over her shoes. None of them looked right. *I'd better check on the kids*, she decided, postponing the shoe decision.

"Wow! You look awesome!" Ian greeted her.

"Really? Thanks," said Carrie, glad for the feedback, even if it *was* from a twelve-year-old.

"Ohhh, pretty," Chloe agreed. "You look like Ariel."

"That's a big compliment. Thank you." If Chloe thought she looked like the Little Mermaid, then she had to be on the right track.

Carrie fed the kids the gourmet take-out Claudia had picked up in town. Normally she would have given Chloe a bath, but she didn't want to wreck her outfit. She read her three stories and tucked her in at seven.

Ian was the one who presented the problem. Sometimes he didn't go to sleep until ten. But that night Carrie was in luck. He'd spent the entire day on the beach and it had knocked him out. At eight-thirty he began to yawn and stretch. "I'm going to go play some Nintendo in my room," he told Carrie.

At a quarter to nine Carrie found him asleep in his bed, the Nintendo control still in his hand. Gently she took the control and shut off the game and the lights. From there, she moved rapidly around the house. She locked every door that led outside plus the inside door going down to the pool. To make extra certain, she put the key to that door in her pocket. She wasn't taking any chances.

Next she wrote a note and left it on the refrigerator. *Dear Ian,* she wrote. *I've just gone to Sam's for a sec. Here's the number: 555-3142. Call if you need me. If you need help fast, call the security guards' number on the phone. Love, C.* The plan was that she'd get home well before

Claudia and Graham and take the note down. But if there was a real emergency, Sam could contact her. Hopefully Ian would stay asleep until she returned and never see the note at all.

"What else?" Carrie asked herself. The oven was turned off. There was no water running. Nothing could go wrong.

Hurrying back to her room, she put on the large hoop earrings Sam had left for her. She barely recognized her image in the mirror. For a moment she had an impulse to go wash her face and put on jeans and a T-shirt, but she resisted it. "Shoes!" she said, snapping her fingers. She checked her closet once again. Sneakers, sneakers, thongs, huaraches, a pair of simple white dressy pumps. Then an idea came to her.

Might as well do it right, she decided boldly as she headed to Claudia's room. Mrs. Ball had cleaned that day and the room was transformed. Carrie opened the door to Claudia's walk-in closet. Her many shoes were neatly arranged on shoe trees on the floor. Claudia and Carrie were both a size seven-and-a-half.

Daringly, Carrie picked up a pair of metallic slingback, open-toed three-inch heels. She hesitated a moment and tried to recall Billy's height. He was about six feet, she estimated. Yes, she could wear the heels and still not dwarf him.

Carrie slipped on the shoes and instantly knew why Claudia loved high heels. They not only looked sexy, they felt sexy. Carrie could hardly believe she was looking down at her own feet.

The heel made her entire leg look longer and shapelier. *Where have I been?* she wondered. *How did I miss all this how-to-be-attractive information that everyone else seems to know?*

Carrie knew the answer to that. She'd never learned these things because her life had practically gone into hibernation in eighth grade, when she'd started dating Josh. She'd settled into a state of largely uninspired contentment. Josh had liked the way she looked, and that had been fine with her. *But that was then and this is now,* she thought fiercely.

The sort of changes she was going through now was exactly the reason she'd broken up with Josh, even before she really knew what she was doing. In the beginning, when she and Josh first began exploring the physical side of their attraction to each other, it had been exciting, thrilling—a time of wonderful discovery for both of them. But they'd been a couple for nearly five years. And in that time they'd grown to be more like good friends than passionate lovers. That special, intimate best-friendship was one of the things she loved about Josh, but it was also probably at the heart of their breakup. Somehow Carrie had sensed that she'd be missing something if she stayed with Josh. She'd be missing the breathtaking, heartstopping romance of being involved with someone like Billy.

Carrie pulled herself out of her reverie with a little shake and hurried to the kitchen. The clock read 9:05. She was cutting it close. With flying fingers, she phoned the car service. *Please have a car available*, she prayed.

Luckily, they did. Carrie waited in front of the house so the driver wouldn't honk for her. The night was warm and starlit—the perfect night for a romantic ride on a ferry.

When the car pulled up, Carrie was relieved to see that Kurt wasn't driving. She would have felt self-conscious about her looks—and guilty about sneaking out.

The car pulled into the ferry parking lot at nine-twenty. The huge, brightly lit ferry was already in the slip. "Take me up to the ticket house, please," she asked the driver, handing him the fare.

As the driver neared the small wooden ticket office, Carrie spotted Billy leaning against the wall. He was waiting for her. That alone made her heart jump a beat.

He wore a Western-style faded denim shirt and black jeans. He seemed perfectly at ease as he stood there daydreaming, one leg braced against the wall, his arms folded across his broad chest.

"Hi," Carrie said, getting out of the cab.

"Hi," he said, giving her a quick glance that was just long enough for her to see his gorgeous smile and miss another heartbeat. Then he began looking off into the distance again.

Carrie was confused. Then it hit her. He didn't recognize her. He'd just said hi to be polite. Girls he didn't know were probably waving to him all the time. After all, he was kind of famous as the lead singer of Flirting with Danger.

Carrie wanted to die. Suddenly she felt terribly self-conscious in her revealing dress, her gaudy spike heels, her new hairstyle. *How could I ever have let Sam do this to me?* her brain cried. *You did it to yourself, you idiot,* she realized. She was still struggling over what to do—slink away so he wouldn't notice? Go right up and greet him again boldly?—when he looked up again and found her still staring at him.

Slowly recognition dawned as three expressions ran across his features in rapid succession: flirtation, confusion, and finally surprise.

"Oh, wow!" he said. "I didn't know it was you at first. You look, uh, so different."

He must have read some of the panic in Carrie's face by now because he hastened to reassure her. "I mean, you look sensational. Very . . . uh . . . very different. I mean, I think you always look good, but now you look . . . taller. Taller, that's what threw me off at first. I guess that's the heels, huh?"

"Mmmm," she said lightly. She was trying desperately to sound cool and provocative, the kind of thing she must've heard Sam do a hundred times a day. But inside she felt shy and nervous.

The ferry horn sounded at that moment. "Last call," he said. "Let's go." They boarded the ferry and climbed up the metal stairs to the top deck. Several times Carrie winced as her ankles wobbled in the unfamiliar heels. Fortunately Billy didn't seem to notice.

Something was uneasy between them as they leaned against the railing while the ferry pulled out of the slip. *Just first-date jitters*, Carrie told herself. All through high school she'd dated no one but Josh. Since coming to Sunset Island, she'd gone out a few times with Howie Lawrence, but had never viewed him as more than a friend. This was her first *real* date since breaking up with Josh.

"So, are you excited about making the demo tape?" she asked, remembering Sam's advice to always talk about the guy.

"Things are going so great for us, between Graham letting us open and now putting together a real pro tape," he said. He went on to tell her about the recording session he'd had that afternoon at the studio. "This guy's equipment is not to be believed," he said. The conversation was normal enough, but Carrie noticed that Billy wasn't really looking at her as he spoke. That riveting eye contact was suddenly missing. That was what felt so wrong, she realized.

After a half-hour's ride, the ferry pulled in at Portland. Billy hailed a cab and they drove to the studio. "How did the concert pictures come out?" he asked.

"Great," said Carrie. "I got one really good picture of Graham talking to his band. I was going to send it into *Rolling Stone* to try to sell it, but Graham spotted it and he's thinking of using it on his next album cover. Can you believe that?"

This had happened just the evening before and Carrie was still elated by the news. She'd decided not to tell anyone, not even Sam or Emma, in case nothing came of it. Now she found herself telling Billy about it.

"That is great," said Billy.

Talking too much about me, Carrie scolded herself. Billy seemed interested, but Sam had told her to talk about him. Make him feel superior, boost his ego. And Sam was a regular man-magnet.

"Of course, the picture wasn't really that great. I'm sure Graham won't use it," she added rapidly. *What would Sam say now? Talk about him.* "I'm sure the pictures you take will be much better. I think men have a more natural aptitude for photography." Carrie felt kind of traitorous, since in her heart of hearts she believed no such thing. Still, didn't this sort of thing always work for Sam?

"You do?" he asked skeptically, holding the studio door open for her.

"Oh, absolutely," she lied.

As soon as they stepped inside, the pulsing sound of blasting rock music nearly deafened them. "I told you the guy has amazing equipment," Billy shouted at her.

Carrie just smiled and nodded. They went down a red-carpeted hall and opened a door. Inside, the room was packed with people. "Billy, there you are!" A short, balding man dressed in an expensive-looking silk knit V-neck sweater and linen pants made his way through the crowd.

"Hi, Sid," Billy greeted him. "Carrie, this is Sid. He owns the place."

"Nice to meet you," shouted Sid. "Your boyfriend is going places. I've been in this biz a long time and I can spot star material a mile away. I spotted Graham way back when."

"Really?" said Carrie. "Graham is really a great guy."

"You know them?" Sid asked, surprised.

Dumb! Carrie thought suddenly. She didn't want Sid telling Graham he'd met her babysitter—who was supposed to be home babysitting. Too late.

"Carrie works for Graham," Billy was already telling Sid.

"Oh?" Sid said politely. "Well, make yourselves at home here. Drinks are in that corner," he said, pointing, "and the buffet is against that wall."

"Excuse me," Carrie said tentatively. "I'm going to get something to drink. My—my throat is kind of dry."

"Go ahead," Billy told her. "I just want to talk to Sid about something a minute."

Carrie thought of asking whether Billy wanted something, but she was afraid to disturb him when he was involved with band business. She didn't want to seem pushy or stupid. She hesitated a moment, but Billy was already lost in conversation with Sid. He didn't even glance her way as she slunk off.

Weaving through the crowd, Carrie realized

she was glad to get away from Billy for the moment. Something wasn't clicking between them and she had to figure out why.

All around her people talked, laughed, and danced. Most of the women were Kristy Powell types: confident, slim, gorgeous, and sexily dressed. Maybe Billy was nervous about being seen with her as his date. He might be afraid that she would seem like a little kid in the midst of all these sophisticated people. He was trying to advance his career here; he didn't need her acting like his junior-prom date.

"What'll it be?" asked a good-looking bartender from behind the table.

"A vodka," she ordered boldly.

"Straight?" he asked, raising an eyebrow.

Carrie had no idea what he was talking about. "Sure," she replied.

The waiter gave her a dubious look. "Maybe you'd prefer it on the rocks or mixed."

Her parents didn't drink. She'd had beers at parties, but not hard drinks. Carrie didn't have a clue as to what he meant. "On the rocks," she said, taking a guess.

The bartender poured some vodka into a short glass full of ice. Carrie gulped some down. Instantly her throat felt like it was on fire. The sensation traveled up, making her nose tingle and her eyes water. "Why don't you try it with some cranberry juice?" the bartender suggested, laughter in his eyes.

He filled her glass with the juice. "That's much

better," Carrie said thankfully. She could hardly taste the vodka at all as she gulped it down fast. "I'll have another."

Carrie quickly downed the second drink. She felt herself relax under the influence of the alcohol. Now she could deal with this situation.

Her eyes searched the room for Billy. She spotted him talking to Kristy Powell. As usual, Kristy was all over him.

"I'll take care of this," she muttered. Bolstered by the two drinks, she walked directly over to Billy. "Want to dance?" she asked him, casting a haughty glance at Kristy.

"Sure," said Billy. "See you later, Kristy."

Kristy shot Carrie a deadly look and immediately grabbed herself a dance partner. She was right behind them as Carrie and Billy headed for the crowded dance area. Kristy looked more gorgeous than ever in a short, form-fitting silver dress. Carrie was thankful she'd listened to Sam and dressed sexily. As the old Carrie, she'd have been no competition for Kristy. Now at least she stood a chance.

Billy was a great dancer, moving easily to the beat. Usually Carrie liked to dance, but she'd never done it in three-inch heels. Her ankles wobbled as she fought to keep her balance.

From the corner of her eye, Carrie noticed Kristy. *She's dancing with that Flash person*, she noticed, seeing Kristy's partner. His dark hair was slicked back in a ponytail and he was expensively overdressed in a silk designer suit. He was so wrapped up in his own performance as he spun and rocked his hips to the music that he barely noticed Kristy.

That was apparently fine with Kristy, because she didn't take her eyes off Billy as she danced seductively nearby. She rolled her hips and threw her head and shoulders back as though she were in the throes of ecstacy.

Carrie saw Billy check her out with a quick, darting glance.

You want to see sexy dancing? thought Carrie. *I can show you some sexy dancing.* After all, she considered, she hadn't watched *Dirty Dancing* fifteen times for nothing.

Bending down, she slipped off Claudia's heels and slid them along the floor to the side. As if on cue, the record changed to a hard-driving rock number. Carrie gave it all she had, tossing her long chestnut ponytail, shimmying her hips, and rolling her shoulders with complete abandon.

Billy followed her lead. He grabbed her around the waist and the two of them bumped, hip to hip, to the blaring beat of the music. Carrie could tell by the expression on Billy's face that he was enjoying himself. Together they were terrific dance partners.

Kristy grabbed Flash's hand and tried to compete. But it didn't work. In fact, neither she nor Flash seemed to know how to dance together. They were strictly solo acts.

Carrie had always been athletic, but even she didn't know where her energy was coming from. Billy went down into a low crouch and she went down with him, shaking her upper torso to the beat. She thought of car commercials she'd seen where the announcer used the expression "turbo-charged." That was how she felt. Turbocharged.

"Whoa, mama!" Billy said with a laugh when the song finally ended. "I didn't know you could dance like that!"

"There's a lot you don't know about me," she said, tossing back her ponytail.

"I guess so," he agreed.

"I'm very hot," she added suggestively. "I need a drink."

Billy followed her to the bar. "Vodka and cranberry juice, please," she ordered. Billy ordered a beer. Carrie threw hers down and ordered another.

"I had a whole different impression of you," Billy told her.

"What did you think, that I was Miss Priss?"

"No," he laughed. "Not Miss Priss. I just thought you were a more . . . I don't know . . . serious person."

"I am serious," she said, sidling up next to him. "I'm serious about having a good time." Another hard rock song came on and Carrie dragged Billy onto the dance floor. They danced wildly again, but this time Kristy was nowhere in sight.

"There's Frank," said Billy when the music ended. "He's our lead guitarist. Want to go say hello?"

"I'll meet you," Carrie told him. "I'm going to get another drink. Want a beer?"

"No, thanks," he said. "Maybe you should slow down."

"I never slow down," she flirted.

"You're the boss," replied Billy casually. But he looked worried.

Carrie got another drink and joined Billy as he stood talking to Pres and Frank. Frank was short and stocky with long, curly black hair. Carrie was electrified to be standing among these three soon-to-be rock stars. Everything they said seemed remarkably witty. She found herself laughing hysterically at almost every comment they made.

The rest of the party went by in a sort of blur. Somehow she lost track of Billy for a while. But she wasn't lonely. One after another, guys asked her to dance. Some of them seemed to want to hang around and talk, but she wasn't interested. The important thing was that Billy could see how popular she was.

What seemed like only an hour suddenly turned out to have been *several* hours. "Omigosh!" she cried as she looked up at the clock on the wall. It was twenty minutes after one.

At that moment, she realized that her head was spinning. She was off balance. But through the haze, she remembered one thing clearly.

The last ferry back to Sunset Island was at one-thirty.

FIVE

Claudia's shoes! Carrie thought, frantically looking around. The shoes had disappeared. Carrie put her hand on her head. She felt dizzier than ever.

"What's the matter?" Billy asked, coming up behind her.

"Claud—I mean, my shoes. I can't find them."

Billy scanned the area. "They've got to be here somewhere. They'll turn up."

"Maybe, but I have to go," she said, fighting back the floaty, dizzy feeling. "The last ferry leaves in ten minutes."

"That's no problem. They start running again at four-thirty. There's a little all-night diner not far from here. A bunch of us are going to go have some breakfast and then catch the four-thirty. Is that okay with you?"

Claudia and Graham were always home by three-thirty at the latest. There was no way she could take the four-thirty ferry. She had to get home. "Sorry, Billy," she said, making her way to the door. "I have to work tomorrow. I've got to be on that ferry. You can stay. I have to go."

As she spoke, Carrie realized she was having trouble getting the words out. Her tongue felt thick. And the room had started to spin. Or at least that's how it felt to her. She reached out to steady herself and toppled over to the side, crashing into Sid. "Jeez!" Sid cried as the glass of champagne he held splashed down the front of his sweater.

"Oh, no!" Carrie gasped. "I am so sorry." Drunkenly, she began trying to wipe the champagne from his sweater with her hands.

"That's all right, dear," said Sid. "Billy, I think you'd better take your girlfriend home. She seems to have gone over her limit."

"I have not," she protested sloppily. "I have no limit."

"Come on," Billy said firmly, taking her arm and steering her toward the door. "What about your shoes?" he asked when they reached the door.

"I don't know," she said. "I can't wait to find them. I have to go. You stay here. I'll be fine." Carrie took three steps down the hall and bumped into the wall.

"Come on, let's get you on that ferry," said Billy, wrapping his muscular arm around her. When they walked out the door, the night air roused Carrie a bit. "The car-service place is just up the block," he said. He looked at her and sighed. "Get on my back. I'm going to have to carry you."

Carrie shot him a goofy grin. "Piggyback.

What fun." She climbed up on his back, giggling. When she was on his back, he jogged toward the car-service office.

"You are so strong," she slurred as he set her down against the front of the building.

"I know, I'm a regular Arnold Schwarzenegger," he quipped. "Don't go anywhere. I'm going to get us a cab."

In a few minutes they were in the back seat of an old blue cab, driving toward the dock. As they neared it the ferry horn sounded. "Uh-oh," said Carrie as she tried desperately to keep her head up. "The ferry is going bye-bye. I'm in a lot of trouble now."

"Can you go any faster?" Billy asked the driver.

"I'll try," he replied, stepping on the gas.

When they pulled up to the ferry, Billy threw three dollars into the front seat and swung the door open. A ferry worker wearing a fluorescent vest was at that moment pulling shut the iron bar that closed off the ferry. "Hold up!" Billy cried, waving his arms as he ran toward the man.

Carrie got out of the cab. "Ouch!" She'd stepped on a sharp pebble. Trying to catch up with Billy, she found herself weaving sideways instead.

The next thing she knew, Billy was beside her again. He scooped her up in his arms and carried her to the ferry. Looking annoyed, the ferry hand held open the bar and let them pass. "You both going, or just the . . . uh . . . lady?" he asked.

"Just her," said Billy, setting Carrie onto her feet. She staggered back two steps, nearly losing her balance. "Oh, shoot!" Billy muttered, "I guess I'd better go, too." He handed the man fare for two and helped Carrie onto the ferry.

Leaning heavily on Billy, Carrie made her way up to the exposed mid-deck of the ferry. With a last blast of its horn, the ferry lurched forward.

Carrie's stomach lurched forward along with it.

"Oh, no!" she cried, stumbling to her feet. Drunk as she was, she was aware enough to know that what was coming next would mean total humiliation. She grabbed the railing and pulled herself along as quickly as she could manage. At the front of the boat she leaned over and threw up into the black, churning ocean.

Almost immediately her head felt somewhat clearer. "Feeding the fish?" Billy teased drily as he joined her. She nodded, feeling woozy once again. He took her arm and sat down with her on a wooden bench.

"You know what, Billy?" she said.

"What?"

"I feel terrible."

"I'm not surprised. I bet you'll feel worse tomorrow."

"Really?" sighed Carrie, sliding down in her seat. "That's pretty cool." She let her head drift down onto his leg and fell into a deep, dreamless sleep.

When she awoke she was lying in the back seat of a car. A strong hand was roughly shaking her shoulder. Groggily, she looked up. A handsome face was looking down at her. But it wasn't Billy. For a moment she couldn't figure out what was going on. Then the fog in her brain cleared just a bit.

"Kurt!" she cried.

"Drink this," he said, handing her a cup of hot coffee.

Carrie took the cup from him. "What the . . . how did I get here?" she asked, dragging herself into a sitting position. "What's going on?"

"Your date, that rock-and-roll guy—what's his name?"

"Billy."

"Right, Billy. He called you a cab when you got off the ferry and I got the call. You were really out of it. I told him I'd make sure you got home okay because I got the impression he wanted to take the ferry back to Portland."

"Thanks," she said, sipping the coffee. As she drank Carrie noticed they were pulled over on the side of Thorn Hill Road. "Why did you stop here?"

"I wanted to give you this coffee before we got home to the Templetons'. But that's not really the reason I stopped. I think you have a little problem."

"What?" asked Carrie.

"When I pulled up to the house, I saw the upstairs lights on. And I could see the figure of a man standing in the window. It looked like Graham."

"Oh, God!" gasped Carrie.

"Emma told me where you were tonight. I didn't want to make matters worse by ringing the doorbell and delivering your snoring corpse to them. So I drove back down here and I figured I'd better wake you."

"I was snoring?" moaned Carrie, shaking her head.

"Like a buzz saw."

"What am I going to do, Kurt? I'm going to be fired. I'm going to get sent home." Suddenly she sat up straight. "What if something happened to Ian or Chloe?"

"Are you ready to go to the house?" Kurt asked.

"I have to find out what happened. Besides, what choice do I have?"

Kurt drove her to the front door. "Here," he said as he handed her a mint.

"Oh, no! On top of everything, I have bad breath?"

"Booze breath," he said. "Try not to stand too close to anybody."

He turned out of the driveway and was gone. With shaking hands, Carrie put her key in the front door and let herself in. The house was dark except for the upstairs lights. "Good night, Ian," she heard Claudia say.

At the top of the stairs she saw Claudia in a long flowered nightgown. Without her heels and makeup, she looked very young and vulnerable.

"Oh, you scared me!" she gasped when she noticed Carrie.

"What happened?" asked Carrie. She remembered Kurt's advice and stopped before she was too close to Claudia.

"Chloe had a bad dream. She woke up crying and then she woke up Ian. But where were you? When we got home the house was dark and locked up tight. We assumed you'd gone to bed."

They hadn't even realized she was gone! "Oh, I stepped out for some air," she lied. "I think I might be getting the flu or something."

"You don't look well at all," Claudia agreed.

"I feel terrible. I even threw up once."

"You poor thing," said Claudia. A look of confusion swept over Claudia's face. "Why are you dressed up?"

"Oh, I was just sort of experimenting with a new look," said Carrie.

"This is the time to do it, while you're young," said Claudia. "You really don't look well at all, though." She moved closer to Carrie. "Let me help you to your room."

Carrie held up her hand. "No, thanks. I'd like to go out and get more air. That seems to help."

"All right. I hope you feel better."

Carrie hurried back outside. The air did quell the nauseated feeling. After a few minutes she went back inside and headed for her room. Dropping her dress on the floor, she crawled into bed and fell, once again, into a deep sleep.

The next morning she woke up at eight. Her

mouth felt like a desert and her head pounded. A cheery ray of morning light was shining annoyingly in her eyes. With a groan, she pulled her sheet over her head and rolled onto her side.

But suddenly she sat up with a jolt. The note! She'd forgotten to take her note to Ian off the refrigerator. Grabbing her robe, she ran down the hall, praying that she was the first one up. At the kitchen she skidded to a halt. Ian was standing there, reading the note. "Did you leave us alone last night?" he asked.

Carrie snatched the note off the refrigerator. "I was going to go to Sam's," she told him. "But then I didn't feel right about leaving you. And, anyway, I felt sick, so I just went to bed."

"Oh," he replied flatly. "You still look sick."

Carrie had never felt sicker. Pouring herself a glass of orange juice, she sat at the kitchen table with her head in her hands. "Want me to make you a scrambled egg?" asked Ian, who had just learned to prepare eggs.

"No thanks," she said quickly. The thought of eggs was completely repulsive this morning.

Chloe walked in from the living room. "You're not feeling well?" she asked, patting Carrie's arm sympathetically with her pudgy hand. Carrie had never felt more guilty in her life. How could she have left these two?

Moving slowly, Carrie got Chloe her cereal and juice. It was lucky for her that Graham and Claudia were late sleepers. If they'd been out late, they wouldn't arise until nearly noon.

"Start getting ready for the beach," Carrie told the kids. "Do you want to go to Thorn Hill Beach today?" she asked hopefully. Thorn Hill Beach was the small, somewhat rocky private beach just down the hill from the house. It was used only by the few vacationers on this side of the island and was often empty. Carrie preferred to go there that day. There would be less of a chance of running into someone she knew. She was in no mood to see anyone. If she could have, she would have curled into a ball and slept the day away.

To her chagrin, Chloe and Ian cried out "No way!" in unison. The public beach wasn't rocky, and it abounded with other kids to play with. From their point of view, it was far superior to Thorn Hill Beach.

"Well, then, how about going to the bay beach for a change?" she suggested. Most of the teenagers who wanted to go to the beach went over to the ocean. Because the bay had no waves, it was used more by families with kids. At least at the bay she wouldn't run into Billy or any of his friends.

"Okay," Ian agreed. "I met some cool guys there the other day. Maybe they'll be hanging around today."

"Do you want help with your suit?" she asked Chloe, who was determined to try to dress herself but who was also still a little awkward at it. It often made getting out of the house very time-consuming and drove Ian wild with impatience. Carrie had hit upon a compromise solution of letting Chloe dress herself for fifteen minutes, and then coming in to rebutton, lace up, or turn around anything that absolutely needed correcting.

"I can do it," said Chloe, as she did every day.

While the kids got ready, Carrie went into the bathroom near her bedroom. "Ugh," she grunted as she gazed at her image in the mirror. Her eye makeup was smeared under her puffy, bloodshot eyes. Despite her tan, her skin was pale. "Very attractive, Carrie," she told herself.

After washing and taking two aspirin, she felt a little better. In her room, she dressed quickly, pulling on her most comfortable, worn tank suit, baggy shorts, and an oversized, man-tailored cotton shirt.

"I did it!" said Chloe, appearing at her door in her favorite Minnie Mouse bathing suit. "And 'neakers, too."

"Good job!" said Carrie, deciding to leave the sloppily Velcroed sneakers alone.

Fifteen minutes later they were driving down the road in a silver Mercedes. One of the fun things about working for the Templetons was that they let her use any of Graham's four cars, except for his new Alfa Romeo convertible. When Carrie was feeling good, she most liked to drive the sporty hunter-green Jaguar. But that day she wanted something large and reliable.

It was early and the beach was fairly empty. Only four families were already there. At the very end of the beach a group of sunbathers lay sleeping on their stomachs.

No sooner had she spread their blanket than the group of boys Ian had met earlier came walking down the beach. "Be back later," Ian said, racing off to join them.

Chloe, too, wandered several yards off to join some small kids who were building a sand fort. *Perfect,* thought Carrie, putting on her sunglasses. *At least I'll get a little break for a while.*

The break didn't last long. The throbbing in Carrie's head had settled down to an even, almost bearable pulse and she was gazing blankly out over the ocean when suddenly she noticed Ian in a heated argument with the lifeguard.

Keeping one eye on Chloe, she headed over to the lifeguard. "What's the matter?" she asked.

Ian was red-faced with anger. "He says I can't swim out to that raft. All the guys are out there." Carrie looked and saw the other boys sitting on the wooden raft. They were all watching Ian argue with the lifeguard.

"He's a good swimmer," said Carrie. "Why can't he go?"

The lifeguard pointed to a sign posted on the beach. It said No One Under Five Feet Allowed on Raft. Dangerous Undertow.

"He doesn't have the body weight to fight the undertow," explained the lifeguard firmly.

"I'm sorry, Ian," said Carrie, putting her hand on the boy's shoulder. "It's for your own safety."

Ian threw her hand off angrily. "Now I look like

a total dweeb!" he shouted in a choked voice. "Those guys are never going to hang out with me again!"

"I know it doesn't seem fair, but—" Carrie began. Ian wasn't listening. With his shoulders hunched, he stormed away from her down the beach. Carrie started to follow him, but the sound of Chloe's voice made her stop.

Up at the sand fort, Chloe and a slightly older boy were engaged in an angry sand-throwing fight. "Chloe, stop that," called Carrie, running to break up the fight.

"He 'tarted it!" yelled Chloe, tears running down her sandy cheeks.

"She's too little," huffed the boy. "She's wrecking our fort."

"She's just a little girl," Carrie scolded. "She didn't mean to wreck your fort."

The two other girls and another boy all appeared to be about five or six. "She can't play with us," said one of them, a plump girl with short black hair.

"Come on, Chloe," Carrie said, taking her hand. "We'll make our own sand fort."

"But I want to play with the kids," Chloe whimpered as they walked away.

"You don't want to play with such nasty kids, anyway," said Carrie angrily, trying hard to remember that they were only kids.

"Yes I do," replied Chloe stubbornly. "Why don't they like me?"

Carrie sat Chloe on the blanket and wiped the

sand from her face. "I don't know, sweetie. They're brats, that's why." Carrie gazed down the shoreline until she spotted Ian. He was picking up rocks and skimming them out into the water. *I'll just let him walk it off*, she decided.

"How would you like an orange?" she offered Chloe.

"Okay," Chloe agreed, her small lower lip still turned down in a pout.

Carrie was peeling the orange, keeping an occasional eye on Ian, when suddenly her heart skipped a beat. She looked back again to where Ian was throwing rocks. Right behind him were the sleeping sunbathers. One of them had just sat up. It was Billy!

Now all of them were getting up and gathering their belongings. Carrie recognized Pres and Frank. And Kristy!

Another dark-haired girl, whom Carrie didn't know, was with them. She realized that they were dressed as they had been the night before. They hadn't even been home yet!

"You sick again?" Chloe asked, concerned by the expression on Carrie's face.

"No, sweetheart. I'm okay . . . well, maybe a little sick."

Chloe hugged her. "I'll make you feel better."

Carrie hugged her back and kissed the top of her head. "Thanks, Chloe, that does make me feel better," she answered.

As the group began walking up the beach toward her, Carrie fought down the urge to run away. There was no place to go. And she'd never get away fast enough with Chloe in tow.

There was nothing to do but sit tight and hope they didn't notice her. Turning her back to them, she continued peeling Chloe's orange.

After a minute, a shadow fell across her. She looked up to see Billy standing by the blanket. "Hi, ace," he said. "How's the head today?"

"Feels like I fell down a flight of concrete steps," she admitted. "I'm really sorry I got so looped. I didn't mean to. I'm not really used to drinking." She spoke the words quickly. They had to be said.

"Hey, it happens," he said lightly. "I hope you don't mind that I left you with that Kurt guy. He seemed like a good guy and he said he was a friend of yours."

"That was fine," she replied. *I don't blame you for wanting to unload me,* she thought. *I'm surprised you're even talking to me.* "How was the rest of the party?"

"All right. I wanted to get back since I left without even saying good-bye to Sid or telling anyone where I was going. We took the four-thirty ferry back and then just crashed on the beach."

"Billy," called Kristy, who had walked several paces ahead with the other guys. "Come on." She looked rumpled but still gorgeous in her tight dress.

"So long," he said, heading toward Kristy.

"Bye," said Carrie.

When he was gone, she hung her head. *That was the final blow,* she thought. *First I make a drunken jerk of myself. Then I appear the next day with no makeup and old baggy clothes. I can kiss that romance good-bye.*

At that moment she realized Chloe was walking back to the kids who were making a fort. "Chloe, come back here," she shouted.

"I want to play with the kids," Chloe protested.

"Chloe, those kids don't want to play with you, so just leave them alone," she said harshly.

Tears sprang to the little girl's eyes.

Instantly filled with remorse, Carrie got up and went to Chloe. "I'm sorry, Chloe. I'm just having a bad day. Don't cry."

"I know. You feel bad," Chloe whispered softly. As Carrie hugged Chloe she saw Billy disappear into the parking lot. Kristy had draped her arm over his shoulder.

Life sucked.

SIX

"You didn't," moaned Emma. "Oh, you didn't." Emma and Sam were listening to Carrie a few days later as she told them about her date with Billy.

"Stop saying 'you didn't,'" Sam scolded Emma. "Obviously the girl *did*. She did get drunk, did barf in front of Billy, and did lose Claudia's shoes."

"Don't forget that I appeared looking like a bag lady on the beach the next day," Carrie reminded her ruefully.

The girls were walking down the boardwalk on the ocean side of the island. It was nearly eight-thirty and the sun was setting. The open-air food concessions, which bustled during the day, had pulled down their gates, and the small restaurants and video arcades were starting to turn on their lights. The savory smell of food from the restaurant kitchens drifted through the salt air.

"I'm sorry," said Emma. "But it's just the worst story I've ever heard. I feel so bad for you, Carrie."

"You two are unbelievable!" cried Sam. "What is the big deal here?"

"The big deal is that I have totally blown my chance with Billy," cried Carrie.

"Give me a break. The guy is not a boy. He's a man. Sort of, anyway. A young man. Don't you think he's seen a girl get drunk before?"

"I guess," Carrie admitted, not relishing the thought. It was true that he hadn't seemed too upset about it when she'd run into him at the bay the next day.

"Of course he has," Sam insisted. "He didn't get that sexy, I've-done-it-all singing voice by hanging out in the church choir all day and night."

"That's part of the problem, though. I haven't done it all and seen it all," said Carrie, throwing up her arms despairingly. "I didn't even realize how drunk I was getting on those vodkas. I'd never drunk anything more than three beers before. I felt so out of my league at that party. That's why I kept drinking. It made me feel braver for a while."

"Until it made you feel like losing your lunch," Emma reminded her.

"I'll never do that again," Carrie vowed. "I still don't feel one hundred percent better."

At that moment they saw Kristy walking down the boardwalk toward them. "Here comes Madam Bloodsucker now," said Sam. Kristy appeared to be heading somewhere special. She wore wide black chiffon pants and a low-cut white halter top. Silver bracelets jangled on both her arms.

There was no avoiding her. Kristy was headed right toward them. "How's the hangover?" she asked Carrie when they were nearly face to face.

"Oh, she feels fine, don't you, Carrie?" Sam jumped in. "This girl can really party."

Kristy smirked nastily. "So I hear. You'll have to excuse me. I'm on my way to meet Billy. He's helping me with an article I'm writing about the band. We're going to try to sell it to *Rolling Stone*. I have some excellent connections there." Casting them a small, condescending smile, Kristy kept on walking down the boardwalk.

"What is the story on that chick, anyway?" asked Sam. "Is she from town, has she got bucks, what?"

"Both," said Emma. "She's one of the few locals who come from money. Not gobs of money, but well off. Her father's a retired judge, I think. Kurt knows her. They went to the same high school."

"Did you hear her?" said Carrie forlornly. "She's going to see Billy."

"She's just a nympho fluffhead," said Sam. "Don't worry about her."

"Kurt told me that back in school she had a reputation as the girl most likely to," Emma told them in a low voice.

"Most likely to what?" asked Carrie.

"To do *it*," Sam said, filling her in. "Nothing wrong with that, if you ask me. I hate the fact that guys hang labels on girls for doing the same things they brag about doing. That double standard really ticks me off. Doesn't it make you mad, Emma, that someone would criticize you for doing what comes naturally?"

"I wouldn't know," Emma said honestly. "I've never done what comes naturally to you. I don't mean I wouldn't. I just never have so far."

"Are you kidding?" asked Sam. "I assumed you and Kurt were hot and heavy."

"We are, but we haven't gone all the way."

"What's the guy's problem?" asked Sam.

"Sam!" said Carrie. "This is private between Emma and Kurt."

The girls stopped and sat down on the wide wooden steps leading to the beach. "It's all right," said Emma. "It's not Kurt's problem. It's me. I know he would like to, but he said he's willing to wait."

"Forever?" asked Sam doubtfully.

"I don't know. He's not pressuring me, though," said Emma. "I'm just not sure I'm ready."

"You love him. He loves you. You're both hot for each other. Why aren't you ready?" Sam pressed.

"It's a big step," said Emma. "It's like crossing a line. And I don't know where things are going with Kurt and me. I'm not sure I want to give that much of myself to something that might not last."

"But you never know what's going to happen," Carrie pointed out. "Look at Josh and me. I thought we'd be together forever. But we're not. Still, I don't regret sleeping with him."

"Why, you little vixen! I was sure you were a virgin!" gasped Sam.

"Why?" asked Carrie.

"I don't know. You have that virginal kind of innocent look to you."

Carrie laughed. "I am innocent, but I'm not a virgin. I remember the day after the first time. I woke up the next morning and I actually expected to be different somehow. I half thought that the world would have changed in some unbelievable way. But it didn't. Everything was the same. Josh was the same. I was the same."

"Except a little less tense, I'll bet," teased Sam.

Emma gave her a playful shove, then turned back to Carrie. "But were you really?" she asked. "Nothing changed?"

Carrie thought a moment. "Our relationship changed. It made us closer. And it was wonderful and warm to have someone to be so close to. But sometimes I wonder if it made us too close too young. Maybe you're not meant to be so attached to someone of the opposite sex at that age."

"How old were you?" asked Emma.

"Sixteen."

"Jeez-Louise!" cried Sam. "You mean you've been doing it for years already?"

"Just with Josh."

"Cripes! I could take pointers from you," said Sam.

"Stop it," scolded Emma. "You make it sound like an Olympic sport."

"There is something kind of athletic about it, don't you think, Carrie?" said Sam.

"I don't know. I'm not an expert," said Carrie. "With Josh it was very soulful and sweet."

"Would you do it with Billy?" Emma asked.

"I'm not going to have to make that decision," Carrie scoffed.

"Don't be so sure," said Sam. "Would you do it if he wanted to?"

"No. I'd do it only if *I* wanted to, and then only if it felt right."

"Would you want to?" asked Sam impatiently.

Carrie sighed. "Yes, I would probably want to. But no, I'm not sure I would do it," Carrie replied.

"You would," Sam insisted with a knowing smile.

"Maybe," Carrie said levelly. For a moment she tried to imagine how it would be with Billy. It would be totally different than it had been with Josh. Somehow she knew it. The physical attraction she felt for Billy was much stronger. She had loved Josh. She might love him still. But Billy attracted her differently than Josh had. Her feelings toward him were more emotional, more physical.

"Well, I don't know what to do about Kurt," said Emma. "I guess if it feels right, I'll do it. And if it doesn't, then I won't."

"That sounds like a good way to handle it,"

agreed Carrie. "You'd remember to be careful and all, wouldn't you?"

"Of course I would!" cried Emma. "I'm inexperienced, not stupid. I don't want to wind up pregnant."

"Or worse," added Sam.

"Or worse," Emma echoed seriously. "I'd better make up my mind, though. Every time Kurt and I make out we get closer and closer to it. I'm starting to feel like a tease and I don't know what to do. It's becoming a real problem. More for me than for Kurt."

"At least you have the problem," said Carrie. "It's not really something I have to worry about anymore."

"Come on, Carrie. Don't just give up!" cried Sam. "I thought you were dead set on changing your image. So, okay, your first time out didn't go so smoothly. Look at me. I didn't get to be so cool overnight. It took practice."

"Modest, aren't we?" laughed Emma.

"Well, it's the truth. I know my way around guys, but I didn't always. I'm going to have to take you in hand and give you some serious pointers. Stand up."

Carrie rolled her eyes, but she got to her feet.

"First off, you're standing all wrong."

"I have good posture," Carrie defended herself.

"I'm not talking about posture. I'm talking about attitude. Pick up your chin, stick out your boobs."

Carrie did as she was told. "I feel ridiculous," she muttered.

"You look hot," said Sam. "But your arms are a problem. They're just hanging there. Always keep them bent. It makes you look like you're holding a cigarette or a drink, even though you're not. You get the cool effect without trashing your health." Sam placed one of Carrie's hands on her hip and crossed her other arm over her body so that hand touched the same hip. "That's better," she said.

"Did you read this stuff in a book or are you making it up?" asked Emma.

"These are tried and true guy-getting fundamentals," Sam said in an offended tone. "Now you have the stance. Let's concentrate on your face. It's completely wrong."

"Thanks. That makes me feel great," said Carrie, still holding her "cool" position.

"It's okay, we can fix it," Sam assured her. "Here's what you do. Pucker your lips as though you're about to give a big kiss. Now relax them a little." Carrie did as she was told. "Excellent," said Sam. "And remember to lick them a lot. Wet lips make guys crazy."

"I don't know about this," said Carrie. "I feel like a dope."

"Trust me. I know what I'm talking about. Now I'll give you my real secret. The eyes. It's a system all my own that I've perfected. You should listen to this, too, Emma."

"Speak, oh great one," Emma quipped.

"Don't laugh. This really works. Here." Sam opened her blue eyes wide. "You look at a guy like this when he says something he thinks is clever. It shows you're really impressed."

Next, Sam narrowed her eyes and looked off to the side. "This one says, 'I'm losing interest, work a little harder.' You use it once you're sure the guy likes you. It makes it seem like you might get away. It hooks them good.

"Now I am about to show you my secret weapon," Sam continued as she lowered her chin and then gazed up at Carrie and Emma from beneath heavy lids. "This look is the killer. Only use it if you're ready, willing, and able. It drives guys insane with lust."

Emma and Carrie gazed at each other in an imitation of Sam's come-hither look. Then they burst out laughing.

"Laugh! Laugh all you like," cried Sam indignantly. "But I'm telling you, this stuff works."

"Are you going to use this . . . technique on Flash Hathaway?" asked Carrie mischievously.

"Oh, yuck! No!" Sam recoiled at the idea.

"You know, he was at the party. He was dancing with Kristy," Carrie told her.

Sam's face darkened. "Really? I bet that little tramp is after my modeling job! Maybe I *will* have to use one of my looks on him, after all. Just the 'Oh, wow! That was clever!' look, though. You can get a lot of mileage out of that one without actually doing anything. It's a great stalling technique."

"I guess it lets you stroke a guy's ego instead of something else," laughed Emma.

Carrie gave Emma a playful slap on the arm. "You're getting as bad as Sam."

"Maybe I'm just growing up a little," Emma replied seriously. "It's like this summer is some kind of turning point for me. One thing I'm sure about: whatever I do, whatever decisions I make at the end of this, my life will never be the same."

Carrie expected Sam to make a crack, but she didn't. She was gazing out at the ocean. "I know what you mean," she murmured absently. *Is she thinking about the future, too?* Carrie wondered.

Leaning back on her elbows, Carrie let her own thoughts drift. All right, so her first attempt at being the new Carrie had been a disaster. That didn't mean she should give up. In a way, the problem had been that she'd been so afraid of the new role that she'd tried to hide behind the alcohol. Maybe the key was to do it straight. No matter how nervous she was.

"Do you really think I stand a chance against Kristy?" she asked.

"If you don't roll over and play dead, yeah," Sam answered. "In a way, I'm in the same position you are. The only reason Kristy would give Flash the time of day is because she's after a modeling job. But I'm not going to just sit back and see what happens. Maybe Flash is only looking for one model. And maybe he'll pick

Kristy if I don't do something about it. I think it's time for me to take a little *direct* action."

"Be careful. I don't trust him," Emma warned Sam.

"I can handle Flash. He's got what I want—a chance to break into modeling. And I'm not letting any twit named Kristy take it away from me. I think Carrie should have the same attitude. Direct action beats passive nonaction every time."

"What do you mean, direct action? You think I should ask Billy out?" Carrie asked.

"What have you got to lose?"

"My pride, my self-respect, and my mind when he says no," Carrie suggested.

"That's what I mean," said Sam with a devilish smile. "You don't have much to lose."

"Aaagh!" Carrie cried, laughing. "You are impossible!"

"I think you *should* ask him out," Emma agreed. "As it stands, you think you're not going to see him again anyway. So there really isn't anything to lose."

"I'm going to do it," Carrie resolved. "I'd really like a chance to . . . ah . . . redeem myself. And this may be the only way to do it."

"Good girl!" said Sam, getting to her feet. "I'd better get going. Mr. Jacobs has another date and he wants me home by ten to supervise the monsters."

"How was the party?" asked Emma as the girls climbed the stairs back up to the boardwalk.

"A living hell," Sam answered. "Can you imagine *me* having to stop kids from *making out* in the *closets?*"

"No," Emma giggled.

"I felt ancient, like I was an old biddy or something. I spent the whole night running around breaking up lovebirds, confiscating beer cans and cigarettes, and generally being a killjoy. I mean, that's what I was being paid to do. So I did it."

"I'm glad Ian and Chloe are younger," said Carrie.

"Yeah, at least you caught Ian one year before the big thirteen. He's still manageable," agreed Sam.

"Not completely, though," said Carrie. She told them what had happened on the beach the morning after her disastrous date. "He was crabby for the whole day," she concluded.

"Poor kid," said Sam. "I had the opposite problem at his age. The kids used to call me Stork, 'cause I was so tall. At the time it really hurt."

"Yeah, I felt sorry for him," Carrie said. They walked on for a while without talking. It was now dark, the boardwalk busy with people out for the evening. A warm breeze blew while the waves crashed steadily against the shore.

"What are you going to do about Claudia's missing shoes?" Emma asked after a while.

"Hope she doesn't miss them until I save up enough money to replace them," said Carrie. "I know she bought them in that nice shop over at the Sunset Inn," she added, naming the most exclusive hotel on the island. "They must have another pair like them."

"What will you do if she misses them before that?" asked Emma.

"I don't know," Carrie admitted. "I just don't know."

SEVEN

The next day, Carrie sat on her bed counting out the money she'd earned so far. In one pile she put fifty dollars. That would be enough to pay for dinner in a restaurant. She hoped so, anyway. If she asked Billy out, she wanted to be able to pay.

In another pile was eighty dollars. Would it be enough to buy Claudia a new pair of shoes? *Not in a million years*, she thought. She'd been fooling herself to think she could ever replace the lost pair. A visit to the shop at the Sunset Inn had made that quite clear. She couldn't believe the prices. The most inexpensive shoes there were two hundred dollars.

Before this summer Carrie hadn't even realized that they made clothing and shoes that cost hundreds, even thousands, of dollars. It just hadn't ever sunk in. Of course, she'd known there was such a thing as designer clothes. But it had never dawned on her that real people actually paid so much money for them. Carrie knew for a fact that Claudia owned a pair of heels that had cost over five hundred dollars!

Carrie remembered the day Claudia had brought them home. Carrie's first reaction was that it was absurd—maybe even immoral—to spend that kind of money on shoes. Naturally, she couldn't tell Claudia that, so she had simply admired the shoes. And though it now made her a little uncomfortable to admit it, even to herself, the truth was that she'd felt more than a little bit superior to Claudia that day. At least *her* own values were in place.

Now, just weeks later, things no longer seemed so clear-cut. She'd learned that Claudia and Graham did a lot of good things with their money. Graham had donated a music scholarship to a college. They gave a lot to charity. Claudia was even chairwoman of the Artists' Coalition for the Homeless. So, if Claudia wanted five-hundred-dollar shoes and could afford them, who was Carrie to judge her?

More to the point, who was Carrie to borrow and then lose them?

"They're just shoes, for heaven's sake," Carrie muttered, gathering her money off the bed. She'd always had a strict conscience. It tormented her when she did things other people might not think twice about. If she snapped at someone unfairly, or even pilfered a pen from someone, she could expect sleepless nights.

"Put it out of your mind," she commanded herself. This hyperactive conscience was something that was going to have to be discarded if the new Carrie was to emerge. "It's a new world,"

Carrie told her reflection in the mirror. "Good-bye, goody-two-shoes."

She moved to her bed and looked at the white slim-line phone on her night table. Graham and Claudia had provided her with her own phone number and unlimited use of the phone. "Consider it part of your pay," Graham had told her. "Try not to call Hong Kong too often, if you catch my drift."

Gathering her courage, Carrie called local information. "Do you have a number for Billy Sampson over on Dune Road?" she asked the operator.

"The listing is under the name of Presley Travis, hon," said the operator before giving Carrie the number.

"How did you know that?" asked Carrie as she wrote down the number.

"It's a small island. It didn't take long to learn who lives over at that address," the operator told her knowingly. "It seems I get at least one call a day from some girl trying to locate one of the fellas at that house. What are they? Some kind of musicians or something?"

"Yes, they are. Thanks," Carrie said, then hung up. *Terrific. I'm about to become one of a zillion groupies who chase the guys in the band.*

"Oh, what the heck!" Carrie took a deep breath and punched in the numbers.

"Flirtation station," answered a familiar male voice.

"Hi, Pres. ThisisCarrieAldenis—"

"Not *the* Carrie Alden!" Pres teased. "Not the original party animal? Not the dance-till-you-drop, go-big-or-go-home girl herself?"

"I made a total ass of myself, didn't I?" Carrie found the nerve to say.

"Look at it this way: you're not the first person who ever got clobbered by alcohol. And, frankly, I've seen a lot worse. A *lot* worse. People who would really surprise you." Carrie appreciated his attitude. Pres was making her feel a lot better. "I suppose you want Mr. Sex Appeal, huh?" he said.

"I guess so," Carrie laughed. "Is Billy there?"

"I'm wounded," Pres teased. "I was referring to myself. But if you insist on second best, hold on." Carrie stayed on the phone and waited.

"Hello," Billy said, coming to the phone.

"Hi. It's Carrie. I'm calling because I was wondering if you'd want to . . . but I wouldn't blame you if you didn't, after the way I got so drunk the other night and all . . . but I was wondering—"

"Hang on a second, okay?" he interrupted her. In the background Carrie heard a male voice shouting something. "What?" Billy bellowed back. "I'm sorry," he said, speaking into the phone again. "Frank is yelling something at me and I can't hear you. Give me one minute and I'll be back."

Carrie took a deep breath. *You sounded like a real idiot*, she scolded herself. *Try not to act like a total pea-brain when he comes back.*

Then, suddenly, a brilliant idea came to her. She would simply pretend that she was Sam. Back in high school Carrie had acted in a couple of school plays. She had a little experience in taking on another character. By pretending to herself to be Sam she could shed the old Carrie once and for all. She'd know exactly what to say and do.

"Hi, sorry." Billy came back on the line. "Listen, what Frank was telling me is that we've been invited to a midnight beach party after our gig at the Play Café Friday. Would you like to come hear us play and then go over there with me?"

"Friday, Friday, what do I have to do Friday?" Sam had instructed Carrie not to leap forward with a yes if Billy asked her out again. And she really did need a minute to think. There *was* something she had to do Friday.

"The clambake down at the beach," she said, snapping her fingers. "I promised to take the kids. Graham and Claudia can't go because Graham just gets mobbed by fans at public events. But it should be over before you finish playing. I'm sure I can get there before midnight."

"Great!" he said. "I still want that photography lesson. Things have just been sort of crazy with us these days, with the new demo and all. We were back in the studio yesterday working on it. We're going to send it out with a press release and stuff like that."

"That is fabulous! That is so incredible. You'll

be rich and famous soon," Carrie said, remembering Sam's advice to act impressed.

Billy laughed, but he sounded pleased. "Calm down. We haven't even finished the demo yet. I hope you're right, though." Carrie heard the sound of more shouting in the background. "I'd better go," said Billy. "We're heading over to the studio to lay down more tracks. It is so great working with Sid's equipment. You won't believe the difference in the sound."

"Well, I can't wait to hear it," she said flirtatiously. "And I can't wait to see you again." Somehow Carrie's version of Sam seemed a lot less cool than the original Sam. *Would Sam have been so obvious? Still, it seems to have worked, she thought.*

"Okay, got to go. Bye!" he said quickly.

Happy with the way things had worked out, Carrie headed out of her room and down the hall. The family had gone out for the day on a private yacht owned by a friend of Graham's. She had the day all to herself. The sound of her phone ringing made her run back. "Hello," she answered breathlessly.

"It's only me," said Sam. "The monsters found two unsuspecting boys to go bike riding with today. Mr. Jacobs actually wanted me to go along, but the three of us practically got down on our knees and begged him to change his mind. Can you imagine? Anyway, I now unexpectedly have the day off and I know you do, too."

"Good. You can help me buy a new bathing

suit," said Carrie. She went on the tell Sam about the beach party. "Did you call Emma yet?"

"She's not available till two. I'll call her back and tell her to meet us at the Cheap Boutique. They're having a big sale this week and they have great suits."

"Terrific," said Carrie. "I'll meet you down there at one o'clock."

Carrie picked up the novel she was reading and headed out to the deck. The drone of Mrs. Ball's vacuum cleaner sounded from the living room. In the kitchen, pans clattered as Mrs. Hanover, the part-time cook, prepared that night's dinner. The Templetons kept such irregular hours that Mrs. Hanover came early every other day, and then just left the meal in the refrigerator. Claudia stocked up on frozen gourmet dinners—or the ever-reliable take-out—for the days when Mrs. Hanover didn't come.

As Carrie crossed the living room, a letter on the coffee table caught her eye. Mrs. Ball had picked up the mail from the post office box in town. At the top of the pile was a letter addressed to Carrie. She recognized the handwriting immediately. It was from Josh.

She picked up the letter and stuck it into her book. When she was settled into a lounge chair on the deck, she ripped it open.

Dear Carrie,

Hi. Was glad to get your last letter. I hope things have settled down between you and your friend Emma. Don't be hard on her. It sounds as if she just didn't want to lose your friendship. You're a special person. People like to be around you, so maybe they say and do dumb things, thinking it will make you stick around. Hey, it sounds like I'm talking about myself, doesn't it? I guess I am. This summer seems so weird without you. I'm used to the two of us doing everything together, so it's hard sometimes. I've been out on a few dates, but nothing special. I know you and I said we were going to stay friends. And I'm trying—I'm writing you this letter, aren't I?—but it's hard. Real hard. You're my friend, but you're more. I miss the more part. Sorry, don't want to guilt you out. But my offer to get pre-engaged still stands if you find yourself interested after the summer is over. I miss the fun we had. I miss touching you. I miss you.

Love, Josh.

Carrie blew aside a strand of hair that had fallen into her face. Josh made her feel so special and loved. He always had. What was the matter with her? Why couldn't that be enough?

Another girl would be glad to have him. He wasn't gorgeous, but he had a nice face and a strong, athletic build. He'd been president of the

Varsity Club in high school, and he'd been their fastest track runner. But he wasn't a superjock, or a macho jerk. He was quiet and thoughtful, and he laughed genuinely at all her jokes. Everyone liked him. And Carrie personally knew of two girls who would gladly take her place.

I've been out on a few dates. Carrie reread the line. It wouldn't be long before some girl grabbed him; if not this summer, then at Stanford University in the fall. How would she feel then? She might be letting the nicest guy she'd ever meet slip right through her fingers.

Closing her eyes, she lifted her face to the warming rays of the sun. *All right, Josh. We'll get back together. It will just be me and you forever.* How would it feel if she said that?

Safe.

Comfortable.

Like a kind of death.

That was the problem. She'd told him they were too young, that they both needed to date a little before they made a decision. At the time she'd thought she was being honest. But now she knew there had been more to it.

Way down, she had known she was looking for something Josh could never give her. She was looking for someone to make her feel the way Billy did. Alive. Reckless. Sexual.

Folding the letter, Carrie slipped it back in her book. She'd write to Josh, but not just yet. It was important to think more about exactly what she wanted to say to him. Instead she turned to her novel and read for a while.

At twelve-thirty she went down to the garage and got into the Jaguar. The letter from Josh had gotten her down. The Jaguar always cheered her up. Soon she was driving along the shore road with her hair blowing and nothing on her mind but the beauty of the clear island bay.

Sam rode her bike into the parking lot of the Cheap Boutique just as Carrie pulled in. The Cheap Boutique was a wood-frame building on the less-chic bay side of the island. It was inexpensive by Sunset Island standards, if not exactly cheap. It did boast a terrific selection of trendy, funky clothing, much of which was very affordable.

In an attempt to hide her wealth, and blend in with the regular kids, Emma had completely reoutfitted herself at the Cheap Boutique shortly after arriving on the island. Sam shopped there so frequently that she was on a first-name basis with the salesgirls. But Carrie had never bought anything there. She'd come with all she needed, half of it from the L. L. Bean catalog, the other half from the Gap. Good, basic clothes—nothing too flashy or remotely daring.

"Got the Jag, I see," Sam remarked, chaining her rented bike to the bike rack.

"I got a letter from Josh," Carrie said as she joined her. "Now I've got the guilts about breaking up with him. I hope I did the right thing."

"Yeah, I guess it's hard," Sam said sympathetically. "I mean, you were each other's first, and all. But, come on, Billy is here and Josh isn't. Besides, Josh is the past and Billy is the future. Let's go find you the most mind-blowing bathing suit on the face of the earth."

They climbed the wooden stairs and stepped into the cluttered store. Posters and Day-Glo art decorated the walls, and rock music blared from the sound system. Racks of clothing were jammed closely together. Hats, scarves, beach bags, and jewelry hung from pegs on the wall.

"Hi, Sam," a salesgirl named Beth called out from behind the register. "What are you on the prowl for today?"

"My friend Carrie needs a bathing suit guaranteed to fry the male brain at fifty feet."

Beth laughed. "Oh, is that all? All our suits are on sale. They're at the back of the store by the dressing rooms. Holler if you need help."

Sam grabbed Carrie's wrist and pulled her to the back. With her keen eye, she began sorting through the rack. "Too small, too boring, bad color for you, oh, yuck, horrendous," she mumbled as she picked through the large selection of suits. Every once in a while she'd pull one out, study it, then wrinkle her nose with distaste and return it to the rack. Carrie felt like a shopping novice as she slowly looked over the bathing suits.

At the end of five minutes Carrie and Sam had each pulled three suits out of the rack. Carrie held up hers to show Sam at the same time Sam held up the three she'd picked.

"You're kidding!" the two girls said in unison.

"Oh, Be-eth," Sam called out in a high, sing-song voice. "I need your he-elp." Beth joined them at the back of the store. "Give us your impression of these suits we've selected, please," Sam requested.

Beth looked at Carrie's suits. "Great suits. Great lines. Comfortable. Great for swimming."

"And these?" asked Sam, presenting her selection.

Beth looked at the suits and then over at Carrie. "Those are the brain fryers."

"Thank you very much," said Sam, taking Carrie's suits and returning them to the rack. "You just saved me twenty minutes of pointless argument. Here, Carrie. Take these suits and try them on. I'll keep looking."

With a resigned sigh, Carrie took the suits into one of the three booths. She closed the wooden door and undressed. The first suit was a leopard print with black mesh down the front and up the sides.

She swung open the door. "What do you think?" she asked nervously.

"Completely hideous," Sam decided instantly. "My mistake. The print is tacky, the mesh looks cheap, and there's way too much bra. It looks like you have highway cones instead of boobs. Next."

"Thank goodness," sighed Carrie. "I was afraid you were going to try to talk me into this one."

Sam rejected the next suit—a black one-piece with a plunging neckline—as being too conservative. Carrie was about to return to the booth when an annoyingly familiar voice pierced the air.

"Why, hello there, girls," Lorell drawled, carrying an enormous amount of clothes toward the dressing room. Behind her trailed Daphne, looking as thin and nervous as ever and holding two or three items to try on. "Why, Carrie, don't you look sophisticated in that little number. *Très chic.*"

Carrie quickly looked at Sam. "I don't think it's really Carrie's style," Sam told Lorell.

Lorell dropped her clothing on a nearby chair. "Hmmmmm, I suppose not," she agreed, critically assessing Carrie. "Here's one that's more your style." Lorell grabbed a one-piece flowered cotton suit off the rack. It had a small frilly skirt around the hips.

"I don't think so, Lorell. Thanks anyway," Carrie said, ignoring the implied insult.

Dragging her clothes into the next dressing room, Lorell began tossing off her own clothing. Daphne went into the third dressing room.

"Don't bother trying on that third suit," Sam told Carrie. "I have just found *the* perfect suit for you." She tossed a red-and-purple suit over the top of Carrie's door.

"That's it, all right!" Sam declared when Carrie emerged from the dressing room. The suit had a neckline that plunged to the waist in the front and back. It was cut high at the hips, revealing lots of thigh and cheek. A purple band at the waist set off the red of the rest of the suit.

"Are you sure?" asked Carrie as she glanced over her shoulder into the full-length mirror. She tugged at the bottom of the bathing suit. "It shows a lot of butt."

"They're wearing thong-back suits this year," said Sam. "That suit looks prudish by comparison."

"I don't know. Maybe if I saw it on someone else, I'd appreciate it more," Carrie said slowly. "It makes me look awfully curvy, though."

"You *are* curvy," Sam reminded her. "If you've got it, flaunt it!"

"You're right," Carrie agreed, determined not to be a wimp. "I'll take it."

At that moment Lorell emerged wearing a pair of black racing shorts and a short cotton top. "Ta-da!" she sang.

Suddenly Carrie had a deliciously wicked idea. A very *un*-goody-goody idea. She pulled Sam into the dressing room with her. "Pretend you want this leopard-print suit and we're fighting over who buys it," she whispered into Sam's ear.

Sam shot her a bewildered expression, but nodded. Sam was always game for anything, even when she wasn't sure exactly what it was she was game for.

"I saw it first," said Carrie, coming out of the dressing room.

"But it will look fabulous on me," Sam protested.

"You'd have to go all the way to New York to find another suit like that," Carrie said, trying to pout without cracking up. "I saw the exact same one in *Vogue* last month."

Lorell watched, wide-eyed, as Sam and Carrie began to tug gently on the suit, each trying to get the other to let go.

"What are we doing?" Carrie said, suddenly softening. "We can't let a bathing suit spoil our friendship. If we both can't have it, then neither of us will buy it. I'll take this red-and-purple one instead."

"You're right," Sam agreed in her best saccharine tone. "You're so wise." The great thing about habitually insincere witches like Lorell was that they never realized when other people were playing the same game.

Daphne stepped out of her dressing room. "These shorts make me look like a hippo," she told Lorell forlornly. "So did the jumpsuit. I am just too fat."

Sam and Carrie exchanged glances. Daphne was as thin as a rail. A hippo was the last thing she looked like.

"Yes," Lorell agreed, to their surprise. "These racing shorts are all wrong for me, too," she added. "Too common."

"We've got to go," Sam said. "See you."

"Toodles, Sammi, Carrie," Lorell said.

"What was that all about?" Sam asked as soon

as they were far enough away so Lorell couldn't hear.

"She is going to buy that suit," Carrie told her. "Watch. She'll buy it just because we wanted it."

"It'll look absolutely awful on her," groaned Sam.

"Exactly," Carrie said with an impish grin.

At that moment Emma walked into the store. From behind the counter, Beth's face lit up. The last time Emma had come in she had spent almost two thousand dollars. And the Cheap Boutique paid their sales help by commission. "Can I help you?" she asked Emma eagerly.

"No thanks," said Emma. "I'm just meeting—oh, there they are." Emma joined Carrie and Sam. They told her about the little charade they'd played out for Lorell's benefit.

"You girls are wicked," laughed Beth, who couldn't help overhearing.

"Total spite work," Carrie agreed. "If it works."

As if on cue, Lorell came to the counter with several items she wanted to buy. And among them was the leopard-print bathing suit.

"Oh, you girls still here?" she trilled. "And Emma, too, I see. Emma, dear, I hope you're not angry with me for having Trenty show up on the island. It was really all Diana's idea." Trenty was Trent Hayden-Bishop III, a boy Emma had dated casually.

One of the meaner tricks Lorell had pulled recently was an attempt to use Trent to try to wreck Emma's romance with Kurt. She'd imported the most obnoxious girl from Emma's old boarding school, Diana De Witt, to Sunset Island. Then the two of them had invited Trent, knowing it would give Kurt the totally wrong idea at the same time they would cruelly and publicly unmask Emma as a rich girl masquerading as a regular kid. It had been the most awful moment of Emma's life, and there had been a lot of hurt feelings and terrible things said before it was all straightened out. Still, it *had* all been straightened out, and Emma was thankful she had true friends she could count on instead of pathetic schemers like Lorell and Diana.

"Diana is dating Trenty now, you know," Lorell went on, oblivious to their obvious lack of interest. "Really, the whole thing was her very own idea. She goes too far sometimes. Half the time I don't even know why I'm friends with her."

Sam whispered in Carrie's ear, "Because bloodsucking vampire bats of a feather flock together."

"Frankly, Lorell," said Emma in her most aristocratic voice, "you, Diana, and even Daphne here are so unimportant to me that I'm barely aware that any of you are alive." Spinning neatly, Emma headed toward the door.

"Well, I never," Lorell huffed.

With a small, insincere smile, Carrie shrugged her shoulders and followed Emma out.

Sam put her hand on Lorell's shoulder and leaned close. "I just want you to know I really envy you getting that suit," she whispered. "It's going to look *fab*ulous on you." Then she hurried out to join the others outside.

As Sam joined them Emma and Carrie were in the parking lot, doubled over with laughter. "I don't believe she fell for it," gasped Emma, falling back against the Jaguar. "Did the suit really look awful?"

"It is the ugliest suit I have ever seen!" Carrie managed to say between gulps of laughter.

"She could poke somebody's eye out with that bra," giggled Sam. "Shh! Shh! Here she comes."

Barely suppressing their giggles, the girls clammed up as Lorell and Daphne walked out of the store. Lorell threw a suspicious glance their way, but kept walking. When she and Daphne were half a block away, the girls exploded with laughter all over again.

"Revenge is sweet," chuckled Sam, wiping a tear of laughter from her eye. "Man, that Daphne is really a strange one, isn't she?"

"She's so skinny, but she thought she looked too fat in the stuff she tried on," Carrie told Emma.

"Maybe she has some sort of psychological problem," Emma ventured.

"You'd *have* to be a mental case to hang out with Lorell," said Sam. "Or maybe she used to be this perfectly normal girl but hanging around with Lorell has made her a nervous wreck."

"If she really does have a problem, we shouldn't laugh," said Emma.

"Her problem is that she's a toady little nobody who follows Lorell around, that's all," said Sam.

The girls had lunch at the Bay View, an inexpensive outdoor café not far from the Cheap Boutique. Then they decided to take a ride in the Jaguar. Emma directed Carrie down a country road that Kurt had shown her on the north shore, which was the less-trendy side of the island and not overrun by tourists.

"Wow! This is beautiful," Carrie breathed as she stepped out of the car onto the dunes overlooking the ocean. "Knowing Kurt has given you a real insider's view of the island, hasn't it?"

Emma nodded wistfully. "The townies mostly use this beach. And the fishermen. Most of the locals live around here." For the next hour the girls sunbathed. Then they went to Rubie's Diner—another unknown but wonderful spot Kurt had shown Emma—for some of Rubie O'Malley's fantastic homemade pie and coffee.

Finally, around five, the girls had to get home. Carrie dropped each of them off and then returned to the Templetons'. She pulled up the drive just as the family was returning from their day on the yacht. Carrie met up with them in the garage as she parked the Jaguar.

"I see you bought some new things," Claudia said pleasantly as she stepped out of the Alfa-Romeo.

"Just a new bathing suit," Carrie said, taking Chloe's inflatable dinosaur from Claudia. "Do you and Graham have any plans for Friday night?" Carrie asked. "After the clambake, I mean?"

"Not right now," Claudia replied. "Do we have anything, Graham?"

Graham was helping Ian untangle his fishing rod. "Not that I know of," he said.

"Good," said Carrie under her breath.

"I caught a bluefish!" Ian told Carrie happily, holding up a plastic bucket. "Do you know how to scale it and everything? I want to have it for supper."

As it happened, Carrie did know how to scale and gut a fish. In fact, she was a pretty accomplished fisherwoman. "Come on, Ian, I'll show you," she said.

As they climbed the inside stairs to the house, Carrie felt nervous but excited. She had her hot new suit. Graham and Claudia weren't going out. *Beach party, here I come*, she thought. This date would be different from the last one. She'd make sure of it. Positive thinking was important, but Sam was right about one thing: direct action was the way to go. No more wimping out.

EIGHT

"We're home," Carrie called in the front door. It was eight-thirty Friday evening, and Carrie had just returned with Ian and Chloe from the town clambake.

"Did you have fun?" Claudia asked, coming to the hallway stairs wrapped in a gorgeous silk paisley-print robe.

Chloe's eyes were bright with excitement. "We had corn on the cob and chicken and hamburgers and ice cream and sodas!" she told her mother.

"What about clams? Did you have any of those?"

"Yuck! Gross me out!" cried Ian.

"I convinced Ian to try a steamer," Carrie explained. "It wasn't a hit."

"At least you tried it," said Claudia.

"Never again," he said, bouncing cheerfully up the stairs. Despite the unpopular clam, the clambake had been lots of fun. Emma had brought the Hewitt kids. Chloe had played well with three-year-old Katie Hewitt, and Ian had hung out with eleven-year-old Ethan. The boys even allowed six-year-old Wills Hewitt to tag along.

Buoyed by the easygoing success of the clambake, Carrie was now ready for her big beach-party date. She bathed Chloe and tucked her into bed. Then she ran to her room and got ready to leave.

With her new suit on she reminded herself of a picture in the swimsuit issue of *Sports Illustrated.* The annual issue always brought out mixed emotions in her. The girls did look gorgeous. There was no denying that. But why, Carrie would wonder, were they parading around in a sports magazine? It wasn't as if they were selling bathing suits, like in a fashion magazine. No. They were simply there for guys to drool over. Something about it made Carrie uncomfortable. It was as if the women weren't meant to be thought of as people. They were just bodies in bathing suits.

Is that how I'm presenting myself tonight? As a body in a bathing suit?

Turn off the hyperactive conscience! she told herself. Her object tonight was to look good. And she did. So that was that.

Over her bathing suit, Carrie put on a pair of jeans and a cotton shirt. "Dweeb city," she said to her image in the mirror. She opened two of the top buttons and tied the shirt ends together in front. "That's a little better," she muttered. After applying her makeup the way Sam had shown her, she was ready to go.

With a spring in her step, Carrie headed out of her room, but the sound of Claudia's voice made her freeze. "I'm going to have to talk to Chloe about playing with my things," she was saying to Graham. Their bedroom door was open, and Carrie could hear them clearly. "I tell her over and over that my clothes and shoes aren't for dress-up but she seems determined to disobey."

"Calm down," said Graham. "What are you looking for?"

"My new open-toed sandals. You know, the ones you really like, with the metallic straps."

Graham laughed wearily. "Oh, you mean the most expensive pair of shoes known to humankind?"

"They're Raffelli originals," replied Claudia, unruffled. "They're works of art."

"Then I don't think you should be walking around on them. Let's just have them bronzed and put them on a pedestal."

"Fine, and we'll just bronze the Alfa Romeo while we're at it," Claudia shot back.

Carrie had heard Graham and Claudia snap at each other several times before. It seemed to her that it happened when they'd been partying a lot. Like little kids, they got strung out and overtired. But now Carrie felt guilty. This fight was over the shoes she'd lost. And moreover, it looked like Chloe was going to be blamed for it.

Then an even more upsetting thought hit Carrie. Why was Claudia looking for her shoes now?

They were supposed to be staying home that night.

Her heart pounding, Carrie went up to their room and knocked lightly on the open door. "Chloe is asleep," she said. "Ian's playing Nintendo in his room. If it's okay with you I'd like to go out for a while."

Claudia looked daggers at Graham. "I asked you to tell Carrie that Phil called," she reminded him tensely.

"You did not!" Graham disagreed.

"Graham!" Claudia shouted.

"Well, excuse me, but I was sure you'd changed your mind. I don't see why we have to have dinner with your ex-boyfriend and his new wife. This guy suddenly appears on the island and we have to put on a command performance. *I'm* the rock star; I don't play command performances for anyone!"

They seemed to have completely forgotten that Carrie was standing there. But it seemed to Carrie that they might not have cared, anyway. Graham and Claudia were not reserved people, to say the least.

"Phil and I are friends and I would like to see him!" Claudia shouted. "*I* have to go to every godforsaken music-business party on earth. *I* have to be nice to record executives who are so banal and self-impressed that I feel as if my brain is going to explode from boredom. But you, the royal rock star, can't do a simple thing for me!"

Suddenly bursting into tears, Claudia rushed past Carrie and down the stairs.

Pulling himself up to his full height, Graham stepped out into the hall. He opened his mouth to speak, then shut it. Instead, he picked up a pair of Claudia's black straw sandals that had been tossed carelessly on the floor and hurled them down the stairs. "You forgot your shoes!" he bellowed as Claudia slammed out the front door.

Graham then slammed the bedroom door shut with a matching crash.

Carrie leaned up against the wall and slowly let herself slide down. Now what was she supposed to do?

From Chloe's room came the sound of whimpering. Carrie went to the little girl, who sat up in her bed. "I'm frightened," she told Carrie, her auburn curls sticking to her tear-stained face. "Mommy and Daddy are fighting!"

Sitting on the bed, Carrie hugged Chloe. "It's okay," she said soothingly. "Do you love Ian?"

Chloe nodded as she rubbed her eyes.

"But you and Ian fight sometimes, don't you?"

"Uh-huh. Ian hogs the videos. He won't let me watch mine."

"So even though you and Ian fight, you still love each other. It's the same with your mom and dad. Once their fight is over, they'll make up and be friends again. Just like you and Ian."

Chloe yawned widely. Carrie laid her down and retucked her covers. "Everything is fine, sweetheart. You just go to sleep now."

Carrie stepped back out into the hall in time to see Graham dashing down the stairs. "Carrie," he said over his shoulder, "I'm going out to find Claudia and take her to this ridiculous dinner. Don't wait up for us." Graham scooped up the black shoes on the stairs and was instantly gone out the door.

"But . . . but . . ." Carrie stammered helplessly. How could this be happening to her? How could it? "Damn!" she cried, slamming her hand against the wall angrily.

Running back to her room, she called Emma. "She's out with Kurt, I believe," Jane Hewitt told her.

Next she phoned Sam. "I can come over, but only till one-thirty," said Sam. "You know Mr. Jacobs has this dumb one-thirty curfew thing. I hate it, but I *did* agree to it."

"I'll have to be home by one-thirty, then," Carrie said. "It's better than nothing. I just can't leave the kids alone again, but I'll die if I don't get to this party."

"Cool your jets, I'll be right there," said Sam.

In ten minutes Sam was at the front door. "Hi, bye," she said, quickly checking out Carrie's appearance. "You look terrific. Have fun."

"Thanks a million," said Carrie as Sam pushed her out the door. "I'll be back by one-thirty. Promise."

In less than ten minutes, Carrie was pulling the Jaguar into the parking lot of the Play Café. The music blared into the warm, star-filled night.

After reapplying her lipstick in the rearview mirror, Carrie hopped out of the car and climbed the wooden steps to the club.

Inside, the place was mobbed. The dance floor was packed with young people dancing to the music of Flirting with Danger, which was playing at an almost deafening volume. Carrie looked around and saw that all the tables were full, so she leaned up against the wall and watched.

A tap on her shoulder made her jump. Howie Lawrence stood beside her. "You here alone?" he shouted, though she could barely hear him.

"I'm waiting for Billy!" she shouted back just as the song ended. Heads turned to look at her. A hot blush burned in her cheeks.

Billy turned toward her also. He flashed her his most gorgeous smile. He held up his hand, his fingers spread. "Five minutes," he said, mouthing the words. Tonight his hair was untied and hung loose to his shoulders. He wore tight, ripped jeans and a faded black T-shirt that was sleeveless and open at the sides, showing off his muscular body.

More people turned and saw that he was talking to her. Carrie smiled back at him, feeling very cool.

"Are you here by yourself?" she asked Howie. She could see from his expression that he was disappointed that she was with Billy.

"I'm with a few friends," he replied. "You're welcome to join us. That is, if *Billy* doesn't mind."

"Don't say his name like that," Carrie objected. "Billy is a great guy."

Howie shrugged. "I suppose. If you go for the rock-and-roll, Adonis, sex-god type, that is. Though I, personally, think that the cerebral, sincere, devoted-love-slave type is infinitely preferable."

Carrie laughed. Howie really was nice, and funny. "I don't see you as anyone's love slave, Howie," she told him. "You have too much self-esteem."

The band began to play again and it became impossible to talk. With a forlorn wave, Howie returned to his table of friends.

Flirting with Danger was even hotter than they'd been at the concert. The smaller venue lent their performance a thrilling edge of intimacy. By the middle of the song, the crowd was gyrating, stomping, clapping, and shouting in a near-frenzy. When their drummer, Si, slammed down the final note, the audience began chanting, "More! More! More!"

The band obliged with another four songs before they insisted that the house lights be turned up. Billy was sweating but exuberant as he joined Carrie. He grabbed her around the waist. "Let's get out of here. We're playing again tomorrow, so we don't have to break it down."

"Great," she said. "I have Graham's Jag." They ran to the parking lot and hopped into the car. "Where are we going?" she asked, pulling out into the road.

"The end of Heron Road," he told her. As they drove, Carrie raved about the performance. She had been truly impressed, but remembering Sam's advice, she poured on the compliments without restraint.

"You're so lucky to work for Graham," he said, leaning back in the front seat of the car. "I mean, look at this car you get to drive. It's a beauty. I've always wanted a car like this."

"Oh, I have one at home," Carrie lied. She wasn't sure why she'd said that. Maybe it was because next to him she felt so young and uninteresting. A Jaguar might jazz up her image.

"You do? Wow." he said, sounding unenthusiastic despite his words. "Turn here," he directed her. She turned the car into an unlit dirt road along which big houses loomed close together, nearly hidden behind high hedges.

"I've never been up this way before," she commented.

"This is where the families who have money *and* live year-round on the island kind of cluster together," he said. "This is it."

Carrie's heart flip-flopped when she saw the name on the open gate at the end of the drive.

Powell.

"Is this Kristy's house?" she asked.

"Yeah," he said, seeming to think nothing of it.

Swell, Carrie thought darkly as she drove up the driveway. *I have to fight the enemy on her own turf.* Carrie reminded herself that she was Billy's date. He was taking her to Kristy's house.

That meant he wasn't interested in Kristy. And that, in itself, was good news.

Unless he's trying to make her jealous for some reason, Carrie worried. Pushing that thought from her mind, Carrie got out of the car and followed Billy around the side of the large house.

As they came around to the back patio, Carrie saw that the party was already in full swing down on the beach below. "Billy! You made it!" cried Kristy in a voice slightly more boisterous than her usual throaty tones. She had just stepped out of the house with a tray of hamburgers and hot dogs. She was wrapped in a brightly colored bandeau bikini top with matching sarong skirt, slit all the way to her waist on one side. "Hello, Carrie," she added as an obvious afterthought.

"Hi," said Carrie, determined to seem confident and unaffected by Kristy's coolness.

Billy took the tray from Kristy as she led them down to the beach. "Daddy's not here this weekend," Kristy said. "So the sky's the limit. Let yourself go."

"Hey, Kristy," called a handsome guy. Carrie recognized him as someone Sam had once dated; his name was Kip. He wore surfing jams, and he had a cooler propped on his shoulder. "Where do you want me to put these sodas and beers?"

"Duty calls," she said to Billy, running a long fingernail along his collarbone. "See you in a bit."

Thank goodness she's gone, thought Carrie, looking at the party scene before her. It was a setting right out of the movies. The moon lit the surf as it crashed against the shore. Strings of colored lights hung from poles, and rock music spilled forth from an excellent stereo system hidden somewhere. It was a jazzy, bluesy kind of rock and roll. The air was filled with the sweet, smoky smell of food grilling on three different barbecues.

There was another, more pungent smell in the air, too.

Pot, Carrie realized. She'd smelled it before at parties, though she'd never tried it. The dumb, dazed look on people who smoked it was always enough to dissuade her.

Carrie glanced over at where Kristy stood directing Kip. Her eyes glistened and she moved in a sort of sultry slow-motion. Very sexy, but somehow off. Suddenly Carrie understood why Kristy's voice had seemed louder than usual. *She's stoned!*

The sound of a pop-top fizzing open caught her attention. "Want one?" Billy asked, handing her a beer.

She was about to decline, but quickly changed her mind. "Sure," she said, taking the beer from him. "I'll take a rest from the hard stuff tonight."

"Good idea," said Billy with a smile. "Are you okay with the fact that there's pot here?"

In high school Carrie and Josh had had a policy about parties where there were drugs. They'd simply left. They'd learned that inevitably the parties just weren't fun. Either everyone stopped talking and just got into their own thoughts, which was incredibly dull, or Carrie and Josh would wind up taking care of someone who couldn't cope with the drug and got sick or depressed or otherwise upset. It wasn't worth it.

You're not in high school and this isn't Josh, Carrie told herself. "Oh, sure," she answered Billy dismissively. "That's hardly a problem for me."

Looking around, Carrie saw that all the girls were wearing bathing suits. So were some of the guys, though some wore jeans and no shirts. Pres joined them. He was wearing a pair of long, brightly colored trunks. "Hey, you two," he said. "Suit up. Get with the party."

Billy pulled off his shirt and Carrie unbuttoned her shirt and stepped out of her jeans. Billy eyed her and let out a low wolf whistle. "Nice suit," he said.

"Thanks," said Carrie.

"Look out ahead, dangerous curves," agreed Pres.

Billy shoved him jokingly. "Hey, go get your own date. She's with me." To bring home his point, Billy put his arm around Carrie. "Let's get something to eat," he said. "I'm starved."

They joined a group of people who were serving themselves barbecued chicken and corn on the cob. They sat and talked with the group as they ate.

Billy was the center of attention. Everyone wanted to know how the demo was coming along. People began asking both of them what Graham Perry was really like. Carrie was in heaven. She had never felt so hip in her life. Here she was, looking like a fox, next to the most attractive guy at the party, and speaking knowledgeably about a rock superstar. Perfect.

Out of the corner of her eye, Carrie saw a few familiar faces. Frank and the two other band members, Don and Si, were there. To her surprise, Carrie saw Diana De Witt and Emma's old date, Trent Hayden-Bishop. Flash Hathaway was there, always hovering near Kristy. She made a great show of fussing over Flash—who looked overdressed, as ever, in striped silk bathing trunks with a matching short-sleeved jacket and too much gold jewelry—but Carrie knew that Kristy still had her eye on Billy.

"Let's dance," Carrie told Billy, pulling him to his feet. The music was slower than it had been at the recording-studio party. During one very slow number, Carrie pressed herself close to Billy. The feel of his warm hand on her bare back, of her breasts crushed against his hard chest, made her sigh quietly with longing.

He seemed to feel the same way. He held her tight at the small of her back, gently pressing his body against hers. When the music ended, he gently ran his hand through her hair. She looked up at him and the next thing she knew, they were kissing.

Carrie felt as if she would melt away into nothingness as she gave herself over to the sheer pleasure of his kiss. She was only slightly aware of the next song as it began to waft through the night air.

But suddenly, abruptly, the music changed. Pulsing, frenetic drums throbbed through the air.

Billy broke off the kiss and looked at Carrie with laughing eyes. "That was sure a quick mood change," he joked.

"Too bad," she said softly. She noticed that everyone seemed to be gathering in a circle to watch something. "What's going on?" she wondered aloud.

"Let's go see," said Billy, moving her toward the crowd.

There at the center of the crowd was Kristy doing a wild, almost ritualistic dance. Her hips gyrated at incredible speed. Her arms were extended and the many colorful bracelets she wore rattled as she danced. Kristy whipped her head around as though she were possessed by a spirit of total abandon. "Kristy took native-dance lessons last time she was in Hawaii," a girl in front of them said.

Just my luck, Carrie said to herself. Grudgingly, she had to admit that Kristy was good. She might not be able to dance with a partner, but alone she was spectacular.

She wasn't sure if it was her imagination, but the smell of pot seemed stronger. It was probably because everyone was standing closer together as they watched Kristy. Around her she saw people passing joints. One came her way. For a quick moment she considered it, then she passed the joint to Billy. He didn't even stop to think, but passed the joint right along to the girl in front of him.

Even though she hadn't smoked, Carrie had the feeling she was getting high just from the smoke in the air. Or maybe it was the beer, or just the headiness of the music and being with Billy.

She wasn't alone, either. There was definitely a feeling in the air. She sensed somehow that the party was about to turn wild in some way. She could see it in the expressions of the faces around her. It was in the air.

And then it happened. Kristy tore off the cotton sarong skirt she wore around her hips. Under it was only the skimpiest G-string bikini bottom. She shook the sarong around herself as she danced and then tossed it into the air. "Take it off!" the boy named Kip yelled in a slurred voice.

Kristy cast the group a bold look, and, still dancing, undid the front clasp that held her bikini top closed. Her breasts looked very white against her deep golden tan.

Carrie couldn't believe it. Casting a quick glance at Billy, she saw that his eyes were glued to Kristy. What was he thinking? Did he like Kristy's wildness? He must. He couldn't take his eyes off her.

"Time to go skinny-dipping!" Kristy cried as she tossed her top high in the air. In the next second she had stepped out of her bikini bottom and was running toward the water.

The idea caught on like wildfire. On all sides of her, boys and girls wriggled out of their suits and headed for the water. The white outlines of their bathing suits seemed to shine in the moonlight, highlighted against their tanned skin.

"Come on, I don't think this is your kind of scene," Billy said. "We can go."

Sure, Carrie thought. *You can drop me home and then come back and be with sexy Kristy. Just like the last time. Well, not a chance.* Carrie tucked her chin and attempted the seductive look Sam had taught her a few days earlier. "I can handle this scene just fine," she said. Then she hooked her thumbs into the straps of her bathing suit and pulled it to her waist.

"Carrie, I don't think this is for you," he said again.

"Well, you don't really know me," she said, meeting his eyes as she removed the rest of her bathing suit. Something in his look made her suddenly feel overcome with nervousness.

"I'll race you to the water," she said, hoping to quell her jittery conscience by a brave show of bold words. Without waiting for an answer, she took off toward the water. What a strange feeling this was, to be running naked under the moonlight! For a moment she reveled in it. If she had been alone, or on the beach alone with Billy, she might have adored it completely.

But on all sides, naked people frolicked in the

water or splashed one another in the surf. Being among fifty other naked people made the whole thing seem bizarre. It had the eerie feeling of a sexy dream that had turned nightmarish.

Panting, she stopped in the surf. With the water frothing up around her, she regained some of her confidence. Being less exposed made her feel more relaxed. She wondered if Billy was still watching her. When she turned, she couldn't see Billy anywhere. He seemed to have disappeared completely. "Billy!" she called.

Flash Hathaway neared her and looked her over with unconcealed lust. "Come on in, doll," he said, running a slippery hand up her arm. "Come all the way in."

Without apology she pushed his hand away. Something had caught her eye. Up by the house, she saw flashing red lights. Then six men with high-beam flashlights came around the side of the house and headed down to the beach.

From behind her someone spat out a curse.

"Police!" someone else yelled.

Total panic seized the group. Some of the guests ran out of the water toward their clothing. Others tried to swim off down the shore. A piercing whistle cut through the air. An officer with a booming voice spoke to the group. "Clothe yourselves and report to the patio. This is a police directive. Anyone not complying will be arrested."

Carrie was frantic. She couldn't let this happen. Suddenly she felt completely ashamed. Desperate to escape, she started running down the shore. The glare of a powerful flashlight made her freeze.

Covering herself as best she could with her arms, she stared into the blinding light. More than anything, she felt like the deer back at home, which were sometimes stunned by headlights and seemed unable to run out of the car's way.

A deep, official-sounding voice boomed out at her. "Miss, please come up here and find your clothes, or we will take you to the station as is."

NINE

Carrie had never felt more humiliated in her life. She sat in the back of the police van tugging at the too-small white towel wrapped around her body. Just moments earlier she'd daringly stripped for all the world to see. Now she wanted desperately to cover every inch of herself. More than that, she wanted to disappear completely.

On all sides of her were other guests in various stages of undress. Like Carrie, most of them had been unable to find all their clothing. Some of the girls had wrapped towels around their bottoms, but wore their T-shirts. Or it was the other way around and they were wearing jeans but only towels on top. Some of the guys, too, wore only towels, or whatever they'd been able to grab.

Across the way, on the other side of the van, Billy sat on another bench. He was in his jeans and T-shirt. His eyes were closed and he sat slouched with his arms crossed tightly on his chest. She wished she could catch his eye, but he wouldn't look at her. The expression on his face told her it might be better not to talk to him at that moment.

The police van drove them down to the station on the bay side of the island. It was a small station, and once the two vanloads of partygoers were inside it was packed.

The reactions of the guests varied widely. In one corner she noticed Pres and Frank, both wrapped in towels and smoking cigarettes. They seemed to be having the time of their lives, smoking and making ironic cracks about almost everything. Flash Hathaway looked ridiculous wearing all his gold jewelry but only a towel. Diana De Witt kept tugging on a long T-shirt as she imperiously demanded to call her lawyer. Trent Hayden-Bishop, on the other hand, looked as though he couldn't care less.

Kristy, who had begun it all, leaned up against the wall, her sarong skirt wrapped around her entire body. She looked dazed and completely out of it. Billy had found himself a chair and remained slumped with his eyes closed and his arms crossed. He seemed determined to make believe that this whole awful event simply was not happening.

Everyone was waiting for one of two phones to call a parent or guardian or friend to come pick them up. That was the only condition under which the police would release them. Up at the front desk Carrie saw one of the officers who had been on the beach. He handed a plastic bag full of half-smoked joints to the desk sergeant. Another officer brought in a large clear garbage bag full of beer cans.

Another officer came in holding a large pile of clothing. "Here are the rest of your clothes, kids," he said in an annoyed voice. "I'm going to hold up each item. Claim the item if it's yours—and only if it's yours."

Tops were easy to identify and Carrie's T-shirt was one of the first to be held up. Happily she took it from the officer and slipped it over her head, still keeping her towel wrapped tightly around her. The jeans presented some problem since many of them were similar. Several heated arguments broke out as guys and girls argued over them.

Carrie was sure she saw her jeans, but Diana De Witt called out for them. Diana had been wearing white pants, Carrie remembered. "Those are mine!" Carrie shouted as Diana was about to take the jeans from the officer.

"They are not," shouted Diana.

"That's it," said the officer, at the end of his patience. "I'm keeping the rest of this stuff as evidence."

"Evidence!" Diana cried, horrified. "Just exactly what are we being charged with, Officer? We were on private property attending a private function. My father is Evanston De Witt the fifth, a partner with the firm of De Witt, De Witt, Pinkston, Harvey, and Rutherford, and I do believe you have an illegal-arrest suit on your local-yokel hands. Not to mention illegal search and seizure and . . . oh, I don't know . . . harassment."

The officer spoke to Diana in a monotone, completely unimpressed by her threats. "Young lady, you and your friends are being charged with disorderly conduct, lewd conduct, indecent exposure, narcotics possession, a violation of the state statute prohibiting the consumption of alcohol by minors, and violation of a local ordinance against bathing on public beaches—you were on a public beach—after sunset. And if you don't pipe down, I might just add littering to the list."

Diana opened her mouth but thought better of it. Instead, she turned on Carrie. "Now look what you've done. Thanks to you I can't get my jeans back."

"Me!" Carrie cried in disbelief. "Your jeans!" It was no use. Carrie turned her back on Diana and went back to waiting on line for the phone.

A quick glance at the station-house clock told Carrie it was two-fifteen. Sam had surely left by now. The children were all alone. When her turn came, she'd have no choice but to call and leave a message on the phone machine. Graham and Claudia might not even listen to it until late the next morning.

A shiver ran up Carrie's back. She didn't know which was worse: the thought of spending the entire night at the station house wrapped in a towel, or the thought of Graham and Claudia coming to the station to get her.

Finally, after a long wait, Carrie got to use the

phone. As she'd expected, the phone machine picked up. "Um, hi," she said in a small, quivery voice that surprised her. "It's me, Carrie. . . . As you may have guessed by now, I'm not home. I'm . . . it's kind of a long story . . ."

"Make it short, miss," insisted the officer at the desk.

"I'm at the police station and I need you to come and get me. I'm really sorry. Bye. Oh, and please bring some clothes when you come. Thanks," she added in a rush. *That was probably one of the weirder messages they've ever received,* she thought ironically as she hung up.

In about a half-hour, Ken Miner, the owner of the Play Café, came to get the guys from Flirting with Danger. Pres patted Carrie's arm before he walked to the door. "Just think of it as another chapter in your memoirs," he said kindly.

"You mean my police file, don't you?" Carrie replied glumly.

"Police file, memoirs, what's the difference?" quipped Frank glibly as he passed by them. "Come on, Pres," he added. "Let's go throw ourselves on Ken's mercy."

Billy got up and joined the others. He spoke to Ken, who quickly glanced over at Carrie. Ken shook his head, then went off to confer with two police officers.

"Farewell, fellow youthful offenders." Pres waved to the group as he left with Ken and the other band members.

"Get him out of here," snapped the desk sergeant. "If any of you other kids think this is funny, think again. These are serious charges."

Carrie was surprised to see Billy return to his seat. He sat hunched over with his hands on his chin. It was time she spoke to him. "Why didn't you go with the others?" she asked, coming up beside him.

"Because my mother raised me to be a first-class jerk, that's why," he muttered.

"What?" she asked.

"Ken is taking responsibility for all of the band members, but I said I would wait here until somebody came for you."

"You tried to get him to take me out, too, didn't you?" Carrie surmised.

"Yep," he replied tersely. "But Ken is smarter than me. He said he's not getting involved with any dizzy broads he doesn't know."

"You don't have to take care of me," she snapped, her pride wounded by his words. "Besides, none of this is my fault."

"Oh, yeah?" He looked up at her angrily. "I asked you to leave. I would have been history, except I waited around for a few minutes to see if you'd change your mind. The police grabbed me at the side of the house as I was leaving."

"Well, go home, please. Don't stay on my account," she said.

At that moment an excited buzz swept through the station house. Graham and Claudia had just come in, still dressed as they had been for the evening. Graham was immediately mobbed for autographs. He patiently signed them while Claudia made her way to the front desk. "I'm here to pick up Carrie Alden," she announced to the desk sergeant.

"Here I am," Carrie said, coming up to the desk.

In all her life, Carrie had never felt so embarrassed, guilty, and ashamed as when she met Claudia's eyes. "What on earth?" asked Claudia, handing Carrie a sundress and a pair of sandals. "What happened?"

Before Carrie could answer, the sergeant handed Claudia a form and a photocopied sheet of paper. "This is a list of all the charges. Please fill out the form and return it to me before you leave. You will be notified of further proceedings."

Claudia's eyes ran down the list. "Lewd conduct and indecent expo—" She glanced around the station house. "I can certainly see that something wild went on."

The desk sergeant cleared his throat. "You rock-and-roll types might think this is a big hoot, but let me assure you that those of us who live on this island don't find pot-smoking, beer-guzzling, sex-crazed teenagers amusing."

"Believe me," Claudia said to the sergeant forcefully, "we do not find this amusing either." Turning back to Graham, Claudia realized that his presence wasn't helping things. In the tiny station house, he was practically being mobbed. "Let's get out of here while Graham is still in one piece," she said. "You can tell us the whole story in the car. Go get dressed."

Carrie ducked into the ladies' room and put on her dress and sandals. On her way to rejoin Claudia, she passed Billy. "You can go home now," she said curtly. "Thank you for waiting."

"You're welcome," he replied, turning away from her.

Graham had some difficulty breaking away from his fans, but soon they were driving home in the Mercedes. "You know what bothers me the most?" Claudia began after almost five minutes of torturous silence. "It's the fact that you would leave Ian and Chloe all alone. How could you do that?"

"My friend Sam was there."

"I didn't see anyone when I got home," said Claudia.

"She had to leave at one-thirty, and I was planning to be back by then." Carrie hung her head. "Of course, I didn't plan to be arrested."

"No, I imagine you didn't," said Claudia. "Care to tell us how you accomplished that?"

Graham spoke up. "Look, it's late. We're all in a bad mood. Let's just go to bed and talk in the morning."

"Am I fired?" Carrie dared to ask meekly.

"We'll talk in the morning," Graham insisted wearily.

When they got into the house they were greeted by a short but very good-looking man and a pretty, petite woman. "Thanks for staying with the kids," Claudia said to them. "Would you like that nightcap now?"

"No, I think Phil and I should get going," the woman replied. "Besides, your au pair already got us one."

Graham and Claudia exchanged bewildered glances, but let it slide. "Good night, Carrie," said Graham as he and Claudia went outside to walk Phil and his wife to their car.

A sort of heavy numbness settled in over Carrie as she dragged herself up the stairs. *Who made those people a drink?* she wondered tiredly, but she was too exhausted to care. Trudging down the hall to her room, she heard the phone ringing.

The phone was still jangling when she reached it. "Hello?" she answered.

It was Sam. "Are you okay?" she asked.

"I don't know. I guess so. I'm not hurt or anything, if that's what you mean."

"Oh, man! I was so worried about you. I hung around until almost two-thirty. I heard your voice on the phone machine, but I couldn't get it because I was upstairs with Chloe, who didn't feel so good."

"What was the matter with her?" asked Carrie.

"The old barfola. I think she just ate too much at that clambake. Anyway, here I have this kid with her head hanging over a bucket and I hear your voice, but I couldn't make out what you were saying. I got Chloe to sleep and I was about to listen to the tape when Graham and Claudia came in. I think they were with another couple."

"Did you speak to them?" Carrie asked, confused.

"Hell no!" cried Sam. "I didn't want to get you in trouble. I hid in a closet."

"You what?" asked Carrie.

"Yeah. I was going to sneak out, but I ran into the other couple."

"Did you make them a drink?" asked Carrie.

"I didn't know what else to do!" said Sam. "It was, like, an awkward moment. So I made them a drink and then left. I thought I could sneak back home, but Jacobs caught me and was he ever ticked off! He's acting like he's my father or something, and he's going to ground me. He'll have a total fit if he finds me talking on the phone in the middle of the night. You're so lucky to have your own phone."

"I may not have it for much longer," said Carrie. "Thanks a lot for staying. It was super-nice of you."

"That's okay. You just owe me for the rest of your life, that's all. But tell me what happened."

Carrie told Sam the entire story. She was glad Sam had called. It was comforting to talk to a friend.

When Carrie was done, Sam let out a low whistle. "Jeez-Louise," she said, "talk about your bad luck."

"It wasn't bad luck, it was my own stupidity," Carrie disagreed.

"Oh, stop hammering yourself," Sam chided.

"What did you do that was so wrong? Did you smoke the dope?"

"No," Carrie conceded. "I did have a beer."

"That's not the end of the world. Next time stick to soda, but you weren't loaded or anything."

"No, I learned my lesson the last time," said Carrie.

"So what else did you do that was so wrong?"

"I got undressed in front of half of Sunset Island."

"Big mondo deal," said Sam dismissively. "It's not like everyone else had their clothes on. Give yourself a break, would you!"

"I hope Graham and Claudia feel the same way you do," Carrie said, fighting to keep her eyes open.

"Yeah, me, too," agreed Sam. "Give me a call tomorrow and let me know how it goes."

"I will," said Carrie. "Thanks again. You're a great friend."

"I know," Sam agreed. "Good luck."

Carrie undressed and slipped on a flowered cotton nightgown. It felt good to crawl into bed. Almost immediately she fell into a deep but troubled sleep. Police sirens, jails, and handcuffs whirled through her dreams. A naked mob chased her and she cried out to Billy for help, but he just stood on the side, gazing at her scornfully. Suddenly he burst out laughing. In her dream she looked down at herself and discovered she was wearing a clown costume and full clown makeup.

She pulled at the clown ruff around her neck, but it got tighter and tighter. It was choking her. "Help!" she cried out. "Somebody please help me!"

Carrie awakened with a start. For a moment she thought she was in her bed at home. Then she came fully awake and remembered where she was.

And what had happened the night before.

It was just dawn. Carrie climbed out of bed and stood at her open window. A cobalt-blue sky was streaked with brilliant, gold-flecked pink. The only sound was the lapping of the waves against the shore. Sunset Island was the most breathtaking place she'd ever seen. Sometimes she'd worried that it would be hard to leave in September. Now it looked as if she might be going home even sooner than that.

Turning to her desk, she took a piece of stationery from her top drawer.

> *Dear Josh,*
>
> *A lot has happened since I last wrote. Some good, some disastrous. Due to the disastrous part—which I'll tell you about when I see you—I might be coming home sooner than I expected. If that happens, and I think it will, I want you to be prepared.*
>
> *It's hard to say this because it might hurt your feelings. That's the last, last thing I want to do. But if I return, I'm*

pretty sure you and I won't be getting back together. Here's why. These last several weeks have shown me worlds I never dreamed existed. I realize that there's a lot I have to learn, and I won't learn it if I have you to rely on, the way I always have relied on you in the past. What I'm trying to say is that it would be the most natural thing in the world to come home and go running back to you. You've always been so understanding, such a good friend. But if I did that I'd always feel that I couldn't stand on my own feet. Josh, you know me better than anyone else. That's why it kills me that I can't even explain to you what I feel inside. It's like there's this passion in me to experience the whole world, but there's another side, too. There's a little girl who wants to be safe and protected. I feel like the two sides are constantly at war and—

Carrie rested her chin on her hand. Maybe she was laying too much on poor Josh. She'd rewrite the letter later. Returning to her bed, she was suddenly very tired again. As the sunrise washed across the room she stretched out and fell asleep.

When she awoke the second time, her digital clock read 10:45. The sound of voices downstairs told her that the household was already awake. *No use putting it off*, she said to herself as she climbed out of bed. She might as well go downstairs and face Graham and Claudia now rather than later. Dressing and washing up quickly, she headed down the hall. Before she was even to the stairs, she heard Claudia scolding Chloe.

"I've told you again and again, Chloe: Don't play with my clothes. They're not for dress-up. But that is not as bad as lying about it."

"I'm not lying," Chloe insisted.

"Chloe, no one else plays with my shoes and dresses but you. I gave you some old ones to play with, but you must leave Mommy's good things alone. Now please try to remember where you left those shoes."

Chloe burst into tears. "But, Mommy . . ." she began.

Carrie came down the stairs and saw Claudia kneeling in front of the tearful little girl. "I took them," Carrie said.

Claudia shot Carrie an aggravated look. "You're not helping Chloe by—"

"I took your shoes," Carrie repeated firmly.

"Why?" Claudia asked.

"I wanted to wear them out on a date," Carrie confessed.

For a moment Claudia's face was blank. "Then where are they?" she asked finally.

"I lost them."

"Carrie! What is going on with you?" asked Claudia in an exasperated voice.

"I can't pay you for the shoes right now, but you can take it out of my salary every week. I was going to tell you, but I was hoping they'd turn up."

"I hate to tell you this, Carrie," said Claudia, "but those shoes cost about what you're going to earn this summer. But, believe it or not, it's not the money that concerns me. I'm sure you realize we have lots of money. What bothers me is that I misjudged you so completely. You had us all fooled. Mr. Randolph assured me that you were the most reliable young woman at the entire au pair convention. When I met you I believed him, too. Apparently you had us all fooled."

Desperately, Carrie fought down the tears that welled up in her eyes. How could she explain to Claudia that the reliable person was the real Carrie? The new Carrie was the fake.

Or was it?

This was all too confusing. "Am I fired?" she asked in a choked voice.

"I don't know," Claudia replied. "I haven't decided yet."

TEN

Graham paced back and forth on the outside deck. Claudia sat at the picnic table with her hands folded in front of her. Carrie faced them tensely, sitting uneasily at the end of a lounge chair. The beautiful morning had given way to a day that was overcast and chilly. It seemed to Carrie that the day reflected her mood perfectly. Despite the weather, they'd come outside so that Ian and Chloe wouldn't hear the conversation.

"I've been trying to sort this out since last night," said Graham. "I agree with Claudia. The number-one sin was leaving the kids. Now Chloe tells me that Sam was here until we walked in. The fact that you didn't leave them counts strongly in your favor."

Should she tell them that she had left the kids once? Carrie decided not to push her luck. Silently she vowed never, never again to risk their being alone, not even for a minute. Of course, she might never be given the chance to take care of them again after today.

"It was still irresponsible of you, though," said

Claudia. "We understand that you didn't plan to be arrested. But you knew Sam could only stay until a certain hour. A million things could have delayed you besides being arrested, and then the kids *would* have been all alone."

"I realize that now," Carrie said sincerely. "I'm really sorry, I—"

"We're not letting you off the hook," Graham interrupted. "But I think Claudia and I have to take some of the blame here."

Claudia looked at him sharply. Apparently she did not agree. "How do you figure that?" she asked levelly.

"Carrie never knows when she's going to have off. She can't make plans and that's probably not fair. Remember, we did tell her we weren't going out last night."

"I know, but that's why we hired her," Claudia objected. "So we could have our freedom." Drumming her fingers on the table, she cast a thoughtful look at Carrie. "This date was a big deal for you, wasn't it?"

"I thought so at the time," Carrie admitted.

"And you did ask us ahead of time," Claudia conceded. "We're a pretty unstructured family, but maybe we're going to have to have some rules."

For the first time, Carrie's hopes soared. If Claudia was making rules, then it meant she wasn't fired. Claudia had seemed much closer to firing her than Graham had.

Claudia proposed that Carrie have every Friday night and Saturday afternoon off. In addition, she could have off when she wasn't needed. Otherwise she was on call at all times. "If we want to go out on a Friday we'll trade you a different night for it, but we'll have to give you two days' notice. Does that sound fair?"

It did sound fair to Carrie, though she would have agreed to anything Claudia had suggested.

"I am going to insist on another rule," added Graham. "I would like you to be home by two-thirty on any night that you're out. Up until now I haven't cared, but I've been wrong. I have to deliver you home safely in September. After two-thirty, whatever is going on probably shouldn't be going on. At least not at your age. I think I owe it to your parents to make sure you're home by then."

"Okay, sure," Carrie agreed readily.

"Which brings me to another subject," Graham continued. "Drugs and drinking. I don't know if you know this, but I lost my first wife to drugs. She was a lovely woman, sweet and innocent just like you, but she didn't realize she was playing with fire. I care about you, Carrie. I think you're a good kid. But I care about Ian and Chloe more. I will not have that stuff in my house or anywhere near my children. That is firm, absolute. There are no second chances on this issue."

"I would never have drugs around the kids," said Carrie, horrified at the thought. "I wasn't smoking last night, honestly. I've never, ever done drugs. And I never would."

"We could see that you weren't stoned," Claudia said. "But even drinking can get out of hand. You have to watch yourself. Graham doesn't drink at all; I have a few when we go out but I limit myself to one an hour."

I learned that lesson the hard way, thought Carrie, but she said nothing.

"Time to talk about the shoes," said Claudia. "I loved those shoes. What the hell happened to them? I hadn't even worn them yet."

Without going into detail, Carrie told them about losing the shoes at the studio. "I figured I'd put them back and everything would be fine. I feel terrible."

"You figured a lot of things that didn't turn out as you planned, didn't you?" said Claudia grimly.

"I guess so," Carrie agreed sadly.

Suddenly Claudia threw her hands up in exasperation. "You don't know how much I hate this whole scene!" she cried. "I'm only twenty-five damn years old. I was your age almost yesterday. I guess I'm angry because you're forcing me to be this major drag of an authority figure. We don't want to blow your good time, Carrie. But I can't have you leaving the kids, taking my things, lying to us. This is my vacation. We hired you so we wouldn't have to worry about the kids. I'll be damned if I'm going to have to babysit the babysitter!"

Carrie felt humiliated. And more than that, she really felt bad. Graham and Claudia had been nothing but nice to her since she arrived. Now she'd upset them. "I don't know what to say. I'm just so embarrassed and sorry," she said as tears splashed down her cheeks. "If you give me another chance, I promise you won't regret it. I don't know what's the matter with me lately. I'm not like this at all. Not usually."

Graham and Claudia looked at each other. Carrie was surprised to see a look in their eyes that bordered on amusement. "I guess love makes all of us do dumb things sometimes," said Claudia.

Carrie wiped her eyes. "How did you know?" she asked.

"It's not real difficult to tell that you and Billy have a thing for each other," said Graham gently.

"You'd have to be blind to miss it," Claudia added. "That's what the new hairdo and makeup and all are about, right?"

Carrie nodded. "I've been a major jerk."

Claudia and Graham smiled sympathetically. "Some of the change has been cute, some of it has been a little extreme," said Claudia. "But I thought you looked real pretty the way you were."

"Billy must have thought so, too," said Graham. "He couldn't stop looking at you all through the concert. As I recall, that was before the new Carrie showed up."

"I wanted to be more like Kristy Powell," said Carrie glumly.

Claudia threw her head back and laughed.

"Kristy Powell!" she cried, still laughing. "Excuse me, Carrie, but you *are* a major jerk."

"Claudia!" Graham scolded.

"I'm sorry, Graham, but Kristy Powell has been out with every boy on this island. And every boy on the island knows it. She's a supergroupie. Remember last summer, when *we* couldn't get rid of her?" Claudia turned back to Carrie and explained, "I practically had to kick her in the butt to keep her away from Graham. That girl is so screwed up. Nobody takes her seriously. I mean, it's sad, really. I'm sure she could use a good shrink. But she's a mess and that's the truth of it."

"Gee," said Graham, holding his hand to his chest and pretending to be upset, "I didn't know all this about Kristy. In fact, I thought she was showing remarkably good taste last summer. I was very flattered. You've burst my bubble."

"Oh, shut up, Graham." Claudia laughed again. "He's kidding, if you couldn't tell. As I remember it from last summer, his exact words were, 'Let's ditch that dumb airhead before she drives me insane.'"

"I said that?" asked Graham, keeping up his pretense.

"Yes, you did."

Graham looked at Carrie seriously. "She's right. I did. Kristy Powell is nobody to model yourself on, believe me."

"But don't you think I could loosen up a little?

I mean, I come across as such a goody-goody. I *am* a goody-goody. But I don't want to be."

"If you want to spread your wings, take it slow," Claudia advised. She shook her head and laughed gently. "At least take it slow until September, when I'm not responsible for you anymore, okay?"

"Yeah, please," said Graham. "We don't want to send you home with an alcohol or drug problem, or pregnant . . ."

"Or with any horrible diseases," Claudia added pointedly. "So be smart and be careful. Okay? And I'll give you some free advice: if it ain't broke, don't fix it. In other words, it's fine to experiment a little, but don't lose sight of yourself."

"Okay," said Carrie seriously.

"Okay," Graham echoed. "Then let's call this a wrap. If nobody minds, I'm going back to bed. I'm exhausted." Looking worn out, Graham left the porch.

"I have a headache myself," said Claudia. "What a hideous fifteen hours these have been. It started with a fight between Graham and me, and progressed into an incredibly uncomfortable dinner with my ex-boyfriend and his new wife. I forgot what a putz Phil could be! Then I had a little pleasure trip to the local station house, spent a sleepless night, and for the last hour got to act like the principal of my old high school."

"I'm so sorry," Carrie repeated. "Maybe you should go back to bed, too."

Claudia got up from the table and headed into the house. "That sounds like an excellent idea. It's too nasty to take the kids to the beach—just keep them reasonably quiet, though."

"Is it all right if I take them into town?" Carrie asked.

"That's a good idea," Claudia agreed. "I'll give you some money before you go to buy them some goodies."

"I have money," said Carrie. "I'd like to treat them. It's the least I can do. Thanks for the second chance."

"You're welcome," said Claudia. "Don't let me down."

"I won't."

After giving them lunch, Carrie buckled Ian and Chloe into the Mercedes and drove toward town. "Where did you go last night?" asked Ian.

"Out with some friends. It was dumb. I'm sorry," she replied.

"You went out the other night, too, didn't you?" he said accusingly.

"I'm never going to do it again, Ian. I promise," she told him.

"Sure," he said sarcastically. "I really believe you. Hey, I don't care if you do go out. I won't tell. I don't need a babysitter, anyway. Besides, I think it's cool to sneak out at night."

I've certainly set a fine example, she chided herself. "It wasn't cool, Ian. It really was dumb."

Carrie parked the car and steered the kids down the street. A light rain had started to fall.

Carrie knelt to put up the hood of Chloe's yellow slicker and tie it in place. The narrow street along the bay was crowded with shoppers and browsers, as it always was on rainy days.

"There you go," said Carrie. As she stood up, she was jolted by the sight of a van parked across the street. It was Flirting with Danger's van. Was Billy around? Would she bump into him? Did she want to?

For the next half-hour she browsed through the stores with Ian and Chloe. At a store called This and That she bought Chloe a Sunset Island T-shirt dress and a pair of pink plastic play high heels that Chloe had fallen in love with. *Like mother, like daughter, I suppose.* Carrie smiled to herself as she paid at the cashier.

Ian found two posters he wanted for his bedroom. One was of a rock group; the other was of two very large, mean-looking wrestlers. "What do you like about wrestling, anyway?" Carrie asked as she searched for the posters he wanted in the large bin of rolled, numbered posters that corresponded with the numbered posters on the wall.

"It's cool," was his only answer.

"That explains it," Carrie said with a smile.

On the way out, Chloe stopped to look at a purple plastic unicorn. Her lower lip stuck out in a pout as she patted the toy on the head. "What's the matter?" Carrie asked.

"I used up my presents, so I can't have the horsie," she said. "Why does he have a horn?"

"He's a unicorn," Carrie explained. "He's a magic kind of horse. *Uni* means one. He's a one-horned horse."

"What does *corn* mean?" asked Chloe. "Does he like corn?"

Carrie smiled. "I think it's another way of saying *horn*."

"Maybe they thought his horn looked like a piece of corn," Ian suggested.

"Maybe," Carrie agreed. She picked up the small toy animal. "Would you mind much if I got Chloe an extra present?" she asked Ian.

"No problem," Ian replied. "She's just a little kid. It's okay with me."

"Oh, thank you!" cried Chloe, throwing her arms around Carrie.

Carrie paid for the toy and gave it to Chloe, who immediately showered it with kisses. "Let's go," Carrie said, holding the door for the kids as they left with their packages. Hard as she tried not to, she couldn't help but keep one eye out for Billy. And then she spotted him. He was across the street, heading toward the van with Frank, the lead guitarist.

He spotted her, too. Their eyes met, and then he looked away. She stood frozen on the steps where she was. *Oh, please come over and say something*, she prayed silently.

As if he heard her, Billy looked back. He began crossing the street toward her.

"Come on, Carrie," Chloe called from the sidewalk.

"All right, sweetie, just one sec." With a darting glance, she saw that he was still coming toward her. "I . . . um . . . have to tie my sneaker," she said, kneeling quickly to fiddle with her laces. It was awkward. She had to stall long enough to give him time to get to her without appearing to be standing there waiting for him.

Just then, a pair of open straw sandals and ten tanned toes with neon-pink toenails appeared before her eyes. "Why, hi," Lorell crooned down at her.

Behind Lorell, as always, stood Daphne, fidgeting anxiously with the zipper of her baggy raincoat. "We . . . uh . . . heard you had *quite* the wild time last night," Daphne said, doing a poor imitation of Lorell and Diana De Witt.

"My, my, did we ever," said Lorell conspiratorially. "Diana told us you were one hundred percent buck naked in that police house. In fact, she said you were the one who got the whole thing started."

"That's not true," snapped Carrie, getting to her feet. A quick glance at Ian and Chloe showed her what she had feared. They were all ears.

Another quick glance over Lorell's shoulder made her heart sink. Billy had turned back. The van was pulling out of its space and driving away in the opposite direction. *Damn you, Lorell!* Carrie thought angrily as she watched the van disappear around a corner.

"Oh?" Lorell asked in a cloying voice. "Which part isn't true?"

"I did not start it. And I was wearing something at the police station," she told Lorell angrily. Placing her hands on Chloe and Ian's shoulders, she began to steer them quickly past Lorell and Daphne.

"Now I remember. Diana did tell me that eventually you put on a dishrag or something," said Lorell.

Ian looked up at Carrie. "It was a beach towel," Carrie said evenly. "And I can't say I think much of your judgment," she added, looking meaningfully at the children.

By now she had moved several paces away from Lorell. "Oh, so you were naked in the police station except for a beach towel, is that right?" Lorell said loudly. Several people passing by stared at Carrie.

Mortified, Carrie turned and hurried the kids down the street. "Why were you wearing a towel in the police station?" Chloe asked.

"Yeah, why?" Ian asked, less innocently than Chloe.

"Because I went to a swim party and somebody took my bathing suit," she hedged.

"And the police were helping you find your suit?" Chloe volunteered.

"You could say that, I suppose," she said. "That's one of the things they were doing."

"Where were the rest of your clothes?" Ian challenged.

Carrie let out a long gush of air. She might as well tell them the truth. She was tired of lying, anyway. "Sit down," she said, stopping at a public bench along the sidewalk. "Did you ever hear the term *skinny-dipping?*"

"You went swimming with no clothes on?" Ian cried. "In front of other people?"

"Well, it was dark," Carrie said, cringing inside. "Very dark. Extremely dark."

"You could have drowned," said Ian with surprising seriousness.

Up until that moment, Carrie hadn't even considered that possibility. But Ian was right. "You're right. And the police made us stop doing it, but then I couldn't find my suit, so I wrapped a towel around myself."

Chloe patted Carrie's arm sympathetically. "Is that why Mommy and Daddy were mad at you?" asked Chloe.

"That was part of it, yes."

"It's okay," said Chloe, resting her curly head on Carrie's arm.

"Yeah, don't worry," said Ian. "They didn't fire you or anything, so you're cool."

Suddenly the sky opened, letting down a torrent of rain on them. Grabbing both kids by the hand, Carrie ran down the block toward the Mercedes. Overhead, a clap of thunder made Chloe scream. "It won't hurt you, Chloe," Carrie said. "Let's get in the car."

Soon they were headed toward home, the wipers slapping the windshield. At the top of their voices they sang the theme song from the *Teenage Mutant Ninja Turtle* cartoon show. Carrie realized that for the first time in days she felt happy and relaxed. Like her old self. *If it ain't broke, don't fix it. Right.*

Who needs Billy Sampson, anyway? she thought. *I certainly don't. I'm better off without him.*

That's what she wanted to believe. But despite her buoyant spirits, a small voice inside told her it just wasn't so. She still wanted to be with Billy—no matter how much she told herself otherwise.

She just wished she didn't have to change herself completely in order to keep him.

ELEVEN

The next day, the sun came out in full force and the sky was a brilliant blue. Ian asked to go to the public beach on the ocean. "Maybe you'll see your new pals there," Carrie said, loading the trunk of the Mercedes with towels, beach chairs, an umbrella, and sand toys.

"I hope not," Ian grumbled.

"Why not?" Carrie asked, slamming the trunk shut.

"They think I'm a total dweeb because that stupid lifeguard wouldn't let me swim to the raft."

Carrie lifted Chloe, placed her in the middle of the back seat, and fastened her seatbelt. "Did one of the kids say something to you?" she asked Ian, who had climbed into the front seat.

"No, I didn't give them the chance. But I know they were thinking it."

"I need my new uni-horsie," Chloe cried out. "We forgot it." Chloe had grown very fond of the toy unicorn Carrie had bought her the day before. She'd hardly put it down since walking out of the store.

"Oh, okay," said Carrie. "Don't you guys move, I'll be right back." Racing upstairs, she found the toy unicorn on the bathroom sink and quickly returned to the car with it.

"Thank you," said Chloe, hugging the toy tightly as soon as Carrie handed it to her.

Getting into the driver's seat, Carrie buckled up and started the car. "I don't see why they would think that," she told Ian, picking up where they had left off as she backed out of the garage. "You wanted to swim out there, but the lifeguard stopped you. It wasn't your fault."

Ian slumped sullenly in his seat, and Carrie decided not to pursue it. She wished she could comfort him by telling him that it was just a matter of time before he grew, that she herself had been one of the shortest girls in her class until sixth grade, when she'd suddenly shot up to her present height.

She glanced over at Ian again as she cruised towards the beach. No, it was better to drop it. His small size was a sensitive subject and he looked in no mood to talk about it, however much good Carrie thought it might do him to vent his frustrations or benefit from hearing about her own growing experience.

Growing up was a lot of pressure—pressure that Carrie had thought was behind her when she left high school. *Who am I kidding?* she asked herself bitterly. *It's just beginning for me.*

It was true that Carrie had been so content—with herself and her long-term relationship with Josh—that it had never occurred to her to try to change. She didn't want to. She'd just sort of stopped growing. *I'm practically the same now as I was when I was twelve*, she thought disgustedly.

She didn't want to have to change in order to attract Billy, but she wondered whether she would feel at such a disadvantage now if she'd been growing and changing all along. Maybe if she had, she wouldn't feel so much like a little girl playing with big kids.

"I love you just the way you are," Josh always used to tell her. What did that really mean? Was it total acceptance of her true self? Or was it just another way to keep her stuck in a rut—or in a relationship? *Why am I feeling so resentful?* she thought. *Like I'm trying to blame Josh or something. Is it* anyone's *fault?*

All the fashion magazines and ads for makeup and hair-care products were targeted at women's self-esteem. It seemed so wrong, all this pressure to compete over whose hair was shinier and had more body, whose lips were fuller, redder.

Daphne was a perfect example. "I look like a hippo," she'd said. Nothing could be further from the truth. If anything, she looked emaciated. Did she really believe she looked fat? Was it because she looked in the mirror and didn't see a fashion model looking back?

How could anyone compete with models who

devoted their entire lives to their looks, who had their hair and makeup done by the best professionals in the world before they stepped in front of the camera? Even then, if the picture revealed a flaw, Carrie knew the photographer could blur it or fade it out in the development process. Or an artist might actually touch it up, hiding blemishes and fluffing hair with an airbrush. Even models didn't really look as good as they looked in their pictures!

But I knew all that, Carrie told herself as she pulled into the parking lot. Still, she'd let herself fall into the same trap. Why?

In her heart she knew why. She hadn't trusted herself. She'd wanted Billy so badly that she'd lost faith in her own judgment.

She tried to tell herself that if Billy wanted a girl who looked and dressed like a high-fashion model, then he wasn't worth it. If he couldn't look past that at the real person underneath, he was too shallow for her to really care about. But she did care. She still felt strongly attracted to Billy. And she didn't really believe he was shallow. Hadn't he always seemed nice? More serious than the party kids who often surrounded him? *That was just your own foolish, wishful thinking,* she told herself coldly. *Trying to make him something he wasn't—just because you were interested in his superficial good looks.*

Shut it off, Carrie, she commanded herself as she unloaded the trunk. *It's a gorgeous day. Stop worrying for a minute and just enjoy the day.*

"Can I have ice cream at the beach?" Chloe asked as they headed toward the sand.

"After lunch," said Carrie.

"Do you promise?"

"Yes, I promise," Carrie laughed.

"Could I have a hot dog for lunch?"

"Yes! I promise, I promise, I promise."

The beach was teeming with people, all eager to enjoy the sun after being cooped up in their houses by the rain the day before. Carrie had to search for a spot to spread out her blanket. "Turn around," Ian said quickly. "Here comes that guy. Maybe he won't see us."

At first Carrie thought he was talking about Billy. Then she realized he didn't even know Billy. She looked up and saw a tall, thin, gangly boy of about eleven coming toward them. He was tanned, had very blue eyes, and wore his hair in a crew cut. "Who is he?" she asked Ian.

"He's one of those guys, you know," muttered Ian, turning his back to the boy. "His name is Ralphie Krumnitz. He's like their leader."

"It looks to me like he's coming over to say hi," said Carrie as she slathered Chloe with sunblock.

Ralphie finally arrived and stood at the edge of their blanket. Ian was forced to look up at him. "Hi, Ralphie," he said.

"Hi," Ralphie replied, sitting right down on the edge of the blanket. "Hey, are you really Graham Perry's kid? Somebody told me you were," Ralphie asked bluntly.

Carrie noticed Ian's eyes dart quickly from side

to side. He was weighing the best response. She had a feeling that these boys were local kids. She wasn't sure which reply would be seen more favorably by them, a yes or a no. Obviously Ian wasn't sure, either.

"What do you care?" Ian evaded the question.

"That means you are," said Ralphie. "Otherwise you would have said no."

Smart kid, thought Carrie, impressed. She began digging in the sand with Chloe, but she kept one ear on the conversation between Ian and Ralphie.

"So what if I am?" said Ian, a challenge in his voice.

"No big deal," the boy replied. "We didn't know you were his kid the other day. But then we found out, and we were wondering why you didn't just tell the lifeguard who you were and make him let you swim to the raft."

The look of confusion on Ian's face told Carrie that Ian had never even considered that a possibility. In fact, one of the things she liked about Chloe and Ian was that they didn't consider themselves special. Sure, Ian knew they were rich and that his father was famous. But that was his father, not him. It was probably a credit to Claudia and Graham that they'd kept their kids so unspoiled.

In a way, Carrie wished Ralphie hadn't suggested that possibility to Ian. If Ian liked the idea, it could be the beginning of a bad trend. "I didn't want the lifeguard to get in trouble," Ian answered sensibly.

Ralphie nodded. *Good answer*, thought Carrie proudly.

"I bet you could get out there today," Ralphie suggested. "The water is so crowded, the lifeguard would never notice that you weren't big enough."

Carrie cringed at the reference to Ian's shortness, but Ian took it in stride. "Maybe I'll try," he said.

"Ian, I don't think so," said Carrie, trying not to embarrass him. "I don't want to get us in trouble with the lifeguard." The truth was that Carrie felt the policy was probably sound. If Ian didn't have the weight to fight the undertow, then he shouldn't try it.

"He won't even see me," Ian argued.

"Ian, please. I'm asking you not to," she insisted.

Sticking out his lower lip, Ian blew out his breath in a huff to show his irritation. "Come on, let's go swimming," said Ralphie, getting up.

Ian began to follow him. "Ian," Carrie called as quietly as she could. The boy turned and looked at her. "I'm not kidding, okay?"

Twisting his mouth to one side, Ian shrugged and nodded. Then he ran off to catch up with Ralphie.

For the next hour, Carrie and Chloe played in the surf and built a sandcastle. Carrie prided herself on being an ace sandcastle maker, creating graceful turrets of dripped wet sand along the walls and elaborate, tunneled moats around the castle. The castle was soon so large that other kids began to join in, adding towers and tunnels of their own.

"I'm making a little house for uni-horsie," said Chloe as she patted together a small, crooked tower next to the castle. Chloe dug out a tunnel and stuck in her toy unicorn. "There," she said proudly.

"The royal stables, very good," Carrie praised her. "I'm sure uni-horsie is very happy."

Engrossed in the castle as she was, from time to time Carrie checked on Ian. At one check, Ian and Ralphie were busy body-surfing into shore. Another time they were tossing a Frisbee on the wet sand. *Good,* she thought. She was sure Ian was happy to have someone besides Chloe and her to hang out with.

"I'm hungry," said Chloe after a while. Leaving the other kids to complete the castle, Carrie took Chloe's hand and returned to the blanket. She dug her wallet from her beachbag and took Chloe up the wooden steps to the boardwalk, where a line of food stands, shops, and video arcades stood side by side. The shops had front walls, but the foods stands were open in front, with gates that came down only at night. That day the people waiting for food spilled out of the concessions onto the boardwalk.

"Where did all these people come from today?" she muttered as she made her way through the crowd on the boardwalk. She'd never seen the place so crowded. With Chloe in tow, she went to one of the three hot dog stands and got on line.

And waited.

And waited.

The line didn't seem to move at all. "Pick me up," Chloe whined. Chloe weighed almost fifty pounds, but Carrie felt sorry for her, having to stand so long, and lifted her up.

It was hot and smelled like sauerkraut inside the concession. Carrie started to sweat and her arms ached under Chloe's weight. "I'm going to put you down for a little while, sweetie," she said.

"Noooooooooooo!" Chloe wailed, wrapping her arms more tightly around Carrie's neck. "I want my hot dog. I'm hungry. I want my hot dog!"

Finally Carrie's turn came and she ordered hot dogs for herself, Chloe, and Ian, and then added another for Ralphie. She ordered fries, sodas, and two large bags of chips. *I am not getting back on this line again*, she thought adamantly, adding yet one more hot dog to her order.

Chloe and Carrie returned to their blanket just as Ian and Ralphie were coming out of the water. "Ah," Carrie laughed, shielding herself as the two boys shook themselves dry like big puppies just getting out of the water.

Ian was beaming, proud that Ralphie seemed to like him. "Have a hot dog," he offered Ralphie, without checking to see if there was one for the boy.

Carrie was glad she'd gotten him one, and glad

she'd ordered an extra since Ralphie didn't hesitate to request another. When Chloe was three-quarters of the way through her hot dog she put it down and announced, "I'm ready now."

"For what?" Carrie asked, bewildered.

"Ice cream!" said Chloe triumphantly.

Carrie's face fell. Ice cream! How could she have forgotten the ice cream? She'd have to get on that eternal line all over again. The thought of holding Chloe again was too much.

"I have to go get the ice cream, Chloe," she said, getting to her feet. "Ian, would you and Ralphie please stay here with Chloe while I'm gone?"

"Get me and Ralphie fudgsicles," Ian bargained.

"Okay. But nobody move until I get back. I'll be right back."

Carrie hurried to the boardwalk. It was as crowded as before, and the lines were just as long. "Hi," Emma called to her as she got on the ice cream line.

"Hi," Carrie called back. "What are you up to today?"

"I'm working," Emma told her, getting in line behind her. "Jeff and Jane are with the kids now. I've been sent up to get ice cream, which appears to be an all-day assignment from the look of the lines."

"Tell me about it," Carrie agreed.

"I have some news that you might find interesting. I spoke to Trent today."

"You did?" Carrie asked, surprised. "What did your old pal want?"

"A date," Emma said matter-of-factly. "He's two-timing Diana, so he assumes I might want to two-time Kurt. 'For old times' sake,' he said. What a snake! That wasn't the only reason he called, though. His father wants Jeff or Jane to represent Trent in case this skinny-dipping things goes to court."

Carrie could feel herself go pale. If that happened, her parents would have to be notified. She might wind up with a criminal record. "Sam told you what happened, I guess," she said, crestfallen. "What a mess!"

"I'll say. Don't worry, though," said Emma, noticing Carrie's expression. "I asked Jane about it. She told me that the neighbors who called the police aren't pressing charges. Kristy and some other girl admitted to buying the pot, so that's going to be tried separately. It looks like the rest of you are off the hook."

Letting out a *whoosh* of relief, Carrie relaxed. "That *is* good news."

"No word from Billy?" Emma asked.

Carrie shook her head. "That's one relationship that never even had a chance. Thanks to me."

"Why just you? It was his fault, too. He took you to the stupid party," Emma insisted loyally.

"Yeah, but he wanted to leave. I wouldn't go."

"Oh," said Emma. "Still, maybe it's not over."

"He wouldn't even speak to me at the station house. I saw him yesterday, but good old Lorell got between us. I have to face it, my relationship with him D.O.A."

"What do you mean?"

"Dead on arrival," Carrie filled her in.

Emma smiled wanly and shrugged. "Maybe it wasn't meant to be. You'll find someone better."

After five minutes the line inched forward two paces. "This is ridiculous!" Carrie sighed. "I can't leave the kids alone any longer. I'll send Ian and his new friend back to get the ice cream."

"Good idea," said Emma. "Call me later. Maybe the three of us can do something tonight."

"All right," Carrie replied as she got off the line and walked back out to the boardwalk. Stopping on the wooden steps, she shielded her eyes from the sun and scanned the area. Where was her blanket? Then she spotted her red-and-white striped beach umbrella. "Oh, no!" she gasped.

She hadn't been able to find the blanket because she'd been looking for the kids. And the kids weren't there!

TWELVE

"Ian, where the hell is Chloe?" Carrie asked frantically, her hands on Ian's wet shoulders. She'd spotted him coming out of the ocean as she raced to the blanket.

"She's with Ralphie," Ian replied. "Hey, did you see me? I swam to the raft and back. The lifeguard didn't even notice."

A blaze of fierce anger filled Carrie, but she couldn't let it get the best of her. "Where is Ralphie?" she asked.

"Isn't he on the blanket?" asked Ian. "I told him to stay with Chloe."

Forcing herself to breathe deeply, Carrie looked up and down the beach. "There he is!" she said after a moment. Ralphie was talking to the boys who'd been with him at the bay beach the other day. Chloe was not with him.

Together, Ian and Carrie ran toward Ralphie. "Where's my sister?" Ian asked Ralphie.

Ralphie looked over to the blanket. "I told her to stay right there," he said.

"Oh, God!" Carrie cried. From that moment on

she felt as if she were in a dream. A nightmare. Everything had a feeling of unreality. It was as if she were functioning on some sort of internal automatic pilot, moving with purpose but without thought. Her entire being was in a state of emergency.

"Chloe!" she called, running down to the surf and slogging through the water. "Chloe!"

People stopped and stared at her. "What does she look like?" a woman asked.

"She's four, brownish-red curls, blue one-piece bathing suit. With Minnie Mouse on it," she added anxiously.

The woman shook her head. "I'll run up and ask the lifeguard to look for her," she volunteered.

"Thank you," said Carrie. A large wave crashed at her feet and made her stagger backward two steps. Chloe could easily have been knocked down. And it was so crowded. A little girl who went down and didn't get up might not even be noticed. Tears sprang to Carrie's eyes.

Carrie ran along the wet sand. "Chloe!" Around her people took up the search, looking around, asking their children if they'd seen the little girl. No one had.

Gazing over the sea of people, Carrie remembered Ralphie's words. "Are you really Graham Perry's kid?" If he knew, others might. What if someone had kidnapped Chloe for a big ransom? Or worse? The world was full of twisted people.

"I don't see her anywhere!" cried Ian, on the

verge of hysteria. His slim chest heaved with agitation.

"We'll find her, Ian, don't worry," Carrie said, struggling to stay calm herself, her eyes moving continually up and down the shore. "You keep looking along the water. Get Ralphie and those boys to help you. I'm going to look around the beach."

"Okay, okay," Ian panted.

Picking her way through the crowd, Carrie looked over to the lifeguard. He was standing on his chair to get a better look at the beach. She stopped under his chair. "She's wearing a blue suit with Minnie Mouse on it," Carrie told him.

"Check the boardwalk," he advised.

Carrie ran up to the boardwalk and climbed onto one of the wooden benches. "Chloe!" she called so loudly that it hurt her throat.

"You can't find Chloe?" said Emma, who had come up beside her. The Hewitts were with her; the family had been about to leave the beach.

"I'll go check the other end of the boardwalk," Jeff Hewitt volunteered. "Come on, Ethan, Wills, help me look." Without another word, they took off at a jog down the boardwalk. "We'll bring her to the lifeguard stand if I find her," Jeff called over his shoulder.

"I'm going to go down to the beach and keep looking," said Emma, hurrying down the wooden steps to the beach.

"Katie and I will check the concessions," Jane Hewitt said, laying down her beach chair and towels. "Where would you go if you were going to wander off?" she asked Katie sensibly as they headed for the concessions.

Carrie saw Katie point to the ice cream concession. *Sure,* Carrie thought hopefully. *Maybe Chloe got impatient for me to return with her ice cream.* She watched as Jane stuck her head in the door, but her hopes were dashed as Jane came back out and shook her head.

Walking quickly, Carrie headed down the boardwalk in the opposite direction from the way Jeff and the kids had gone. Her heart was in her throat as she looked from side to side. She was searching so intently that she never noticed Billy running up after her.

"Carrie," he called when he was nearly behind her. "I have to talk to you. I need my—"

"Huh? Oh, Billy," she said with a start.

"I need to come by and get my camera," he said.

She looked at him blankly. It was as if her mind couldn't process his words. "Sure, whatever," she said. "I can't talk to you now, Billy. I have to find Chloe. You haven't seen a little girl with reddish curls in a blue Minnie Mouse suit, have you?"

"Shoot, you mean Chloe is lost?" he said. "I'll help you look."

"Okay. I'm going to keep going down the boardwalk. I don't know where else to look," she said, heading off again.

Billy ran on ahead. She caught up to him when they were nearly to the end of the boardwalk.

Over to their right was Juggler's Wharf. It was a spot where mimes and jugglers entertained the crowds and then passed the hat. Today a crowd was gathering watching something that Carrie couldn't see.

To the left was a long, narrow pier where small motorboats were tied up. "Go check that crowd on the wharf," she instructed Billy. "I'll go down to the pier."

Both of them took off at a run in their different directions. Carrie ran to the middle of the pier. It was wide open. There was little place for Chloe to hide, so there was no sense going further.

A gentle thud made her look down into the water. It was just the sound of a small motorboat bumping into the pier. She was about to look away when something purple caught her eye.

It was Chloe's purple unicorn. And it was floating in the water.

Panic and horror surged up inside her. Chloe had fallen in. Or been abducted by someone in a boat.

Kicking off her sandals, Carrie jumped into the water. She swam out a few feet, then dove down. Perhaps Chloe had fallen and gotten hung up in a boat's propeller or underneath its hull. With her lungs bursting for air, she swam from boat to boat, staying under as long as she could. Maybe it had just happened. Carrie had taken a course in CPR and mouth-to-mouth resuscitation. If she could find her in time, maybe it wasn't too late.

Carrie came up for air a third time. Breathless,

she hung on the end of a boat. Then she saw something, and for a moment she thought it wasn't real. But it was. Standing on the pier, looking down at her, was Chloe.

Billy stood beside her. "She was watching a puppet show," he said.

Kneeling down, he extended his hand and pulled Carrie out of the water. Carrie knelt in front of Chloe and held her tight. Tears gushed down her cheeks. She let them wash over her, not even trying to control them. After a moment, she wiped her eyes with the palms of her hands.

"Don't cry," said Chloe, patting Carrie's wet hair. "I'm all right."

"I'm crying because I'm happy to see you," Carrie sniffled. "Chloe, how did you get all the way down here?"

"I wanted to meet you at the ice cream place. But you weren't there. Then I couldn't find the blanket. I kept walking and walking and walking and walking and walking and walking—"

"So I see," Carrie interrupted.

Suddenly Chloe's face lit up and she pointed to the water. "My uni-horsie!" she cried. "I dropped him and he floated away. He came back to me. Get him, please."

Lying on her stomach, Carrie fished the toy unicorn from the water. "Here he is," she said.

"You thought she fell in, didn't you?" Billy said, sizing up the situation.

Carrie gulped and nodded. She still felt terribly shaky. "I don't know what I would have done. I'd have lost my mind if she had drowned."

"I wouldn't have drowned," Chloe told her seriously. "I would have swum all the way home. I came down here to look for you. I leaned over to see the boats and I dropped my uni-horsie. I almost cried. Then I went back to keep looking for you, but I stopped to watch the puppet show."

"She didn't want to come with me at first but I told her I was with you," said Billy.

"Good girl, Chloe," said Carrie, taking her hand. "Next time, don't go with stranger even if they say they know me. You don't go with anyone you don't know."

"I know," said Chloe as they walked up the pier. "Mommy told me that, too. But he looked nice to me."

"It doesn't matter," Carrie said firmly. "Don't go with anyone, whether they look nice or not."

"Okay," Chloe agreed.

Carrie looked at Billy. "Thank you," she said.

A look of unease crossed his handsome face. "No problem. I, uh, I have to go. See you."

"See you!" she said to his back as he took off up the pier.

"Come on, Chloe, get up on my back," said Carrie, kneeling so she could climb on. "We have to tell everyone you're okay."

Alternately jogging and walking, Carrie made it back to the center of the boardwalk. She didn't see Emma or the Hewitts, so she brought Chloe down to the lifeguard station. "Would you blow your whistle and hold her up so everyone knows I've found her?" she asked the lifeguard.

"Gladly," said the lifeguard with a smile. Chloe looked at Carrie nervously as the lifeguard lifted her and blew his whistle. In minutes, Ian and his new pals, Emma, and the Hewitts all gathered by the lifeguard station.

"Thank goodness!" said Jane, running her hand fondly across the top of Katie's hair. Carrie could see that the very thought of losing a child had shaken her up.

After telling everyone what had happened, Carrie thanked them all for helping with the search. She said good-bye to Emma and the Hewitts and headed back to the blanket to gather their things and go home. Carrie had suddenly lost her desire to be at the beach. "Come on, Ian," she called when she was several paces from the lifeguard station.

Ian wasn't paying any attention. He was in the middle of a heated argument with Ralphie. "Ian," Carrie called at the same moment that Ian shoved Ralphie back hard.

Taking Chloe's hand, Carrie hurried back toward Ian. "It's not my fault," she heard Ralphie shout. "I told her to stay where she was."

"She's just a little kid," Ian shouted back, red-faced with anger. "You were supposed to watch her."

"*You* were supposed to watch her!" Carrie said, coming up behind Ian. "She's your sister, not Ralphie's. I left *you* in charge, not Ralphie."

Ian whirled around and faced her. "You should talk!" he shouted. "You do it all the time. You leave us when you're supposed to be watching us. You did it twice already!"

Carrie was speechless. She couldn't even defend herself by saying she'd left Sam in charge the last time. After all, that's exactly what Ian had done. He'd left Ralphie in charge.

"Well, I was wrong to do that, Ian," Carrie said finally. "And you were wrong to leave Ralphie in charge. Now, come on, let's go home."

"I'm sorry I pushed you," Ian said sullenly to Ralphie.

"No problem, man," Ralphie replied "I'm sorry I left your sister there. I thought she'd stay where she was. See ya tomorrow, maybe."

"Yeah, maybe," said Ian. "So long."

Ian and Carrie didn't say much as they gathered their belongings. They were both emotionally drained. Chloe picked up on their mood and played quietly with her unicorn in the sand until they were ready to leave.

As they drove home, Carrie felt her spirits sink lower and lower. It had occurred to her that when Ian and Chloe told their parents what had happened, it would be the last straw. She could ask them not to tell, but that seemed wrong to her.

So this was it. Her summer at Sunset Island was over. She shook her head sadly. Who would ever had guessed that out of inexperienced Emma, wild Sam, and sensible Carrie, it would be Carrie who blew it? *I certainly wouldn't have thought it,* she thought as she pulled up the drive and into the garage. *Hell, even Lorell hasn't gotten kicked out! I wanted to be a new me and I did it. The new, screw-up Carrie.*

Getting out of the car, she unloaded the beach things from the trunk. "Ian, would you hang up these towels for me?" she requested, holding out the sandy towels with one arm as she continued gathering other items. When Ian didn't answer she turned to look for him. "Ian? Chloe?" They had been standing right next to her a second earlier.

"Not again," she muttered as she checked around the garage. In a moment she found them sitting in the back seat of the car together, talking seriously. "What are you two doing?" she asked, opening the back door.

"Ian doesn't want me to tell that I was lost today," said Chloe. "He doesn't want Mommy and Daddy to be mad at you."

"I figured you're kind of in trouble already," Ian explained. "I don't want you to get fired or anything. And Chloe's okay. Nothing happened to her."

"Something could have. We were very, very lucky," Carrie pointed out, surprised to find a lump coming to her throat.

"I know, and neither of us will ever leave her alone again. Mom and Dad don't have to know about it. If you get fired they might hire some new, geeky person who'll ruin our whole entire summer," Ian said. "You should have seen the woman who took care of us last summer. Chloe, you remember Hannah, don't you?"

"Bigfoot!" Chloe cried, her eyes wide with alarm.

"She always wore these big black shoes, even on the beach," Ian explained. "Hannah wouldn't let us do anything. It was the worst summer of my life. If you go, they might even call Hannah up again."

"Oh, no," cried Chloe, clapping her two hands to her pudgy cheeks and slowly dragging them towards her chin so that the bottoms of her eyelids were pulled down.

The sight made Carrie laugh. "I wouldn't want that to happen," she chuckled lightly.

"Me neither," said Ian. "So if it's okay with you, I don't think we should tell Mom and Dad."

"Uh-uh," Chloe agreed, shaking her head vigorously.

"All right. But we'll both promise to be more responsible for the rest of this summer. Deal?" Carrie asked, sticking out her hand to Ian.

"Deal," Ian replied, shaking. "I promise, Carrie."

Inside, Carrie was climbing the stairs with Chloe, headed for the bathtub, when Claudia called to her from the living room. "There was a phone call for you," she said, coming to the stairs dressed in shorts, a T-shirt, and red cowboy boots. "Billy Sampson called and said he wants to pick up his camera tonight. He wasn't sure when he would get here, but it'll be sometime after eight o'clock. He said you could just leave it by the front door." Claudia looked at Carrie sympathetically. "I'm sure it would be safe there if you don't want to see him. Or I could give it to him, if you like."

Carrie smiled ruefully. "Either way," she said with a shrug. "It's pretty clear that he doesn't want to see me."

"The island is full of boys," Claudia said kindly.

Carrie nodded. *But there's only one Billy,* she thought as she trudged the rest of the way up the stairs.

THIRTEEN

Carrie held Billy's camera in her hands. Once she had given it back there would be no more reason for them to communicate. Their romance—which had never really begun—would definitely be over.

Might as well use it one last time before he gets here, Carrie decided. Claudia had given Carrie the evening off, saying she wanted to spend some quiet time with the kids. Emma and Sam had called, but Carrie didn't feel like going out. The last few days had been emotionally and physically draining. She just wanted to be alone.

At seven o'clock she loaded the camera with a fresh roll of film. She placed it in her beachbag along with her box of stationery, her novel, and a beach towel. Buttoning up her drop-waisted blue cotton sundress and slipping into her huarache sandals, she headed out of the house and down toward Thorn Hill Beach.

The beach was at the bottom of a bluff. A long wooden staircase was the only access point. Carrie made her way down, stopping to look at the blue cornflowers and graceful orange daylilies that grew up along the sides of the railing.

At the bottom, she found the beach was empty. This wasn't surprising. Thorn Hill Beach was usually empty in the evenings. That was one of the reasons she'd chosen it.

Carrie spread her blanket and sat, hugging her knees. The surf pounded against the large boulders that sat several yards out, spraying water high into the air. At the water's edge, long-legged sea birds hunted for food washed in by the tide. They seemed to play a game of tag with the water as it swept in and then ebbed back out to sea.

She picked up her stationery and began a new letter to Josh.

> *Dear Josh,*
>
> *It's almost impossible to describe how beautiful this island is. No matter where you turn there is another scene calling out to be photographed. I don't know where to begin. Should I get up close to a wildflower, or stand back and take in the length of a winding country road with its stone fence and old barn off to the side?*
>
> *The other day, I wrote you a letter which I'll stick inside this envelope. I meant everything I said; I just want to say a few more things. Today I almost lost Chloe at the beach. For a moment I*

thought she'd drowned. That would be the most completely devastating thing I could imagine happening.

Remember when you were reading books about Zen and you explained to me about satori, *a moment of sudden illumination? I think I had a sort of* satori *on the dock today. It was the moment when Chloe stood in front of me and I realized she was all right.*

What did I realize? It's kind of hard to put into words, but I'll try. I realized that all the things I've been concerning myself with lately—my looks, my image—don't matter. Chloe matters. My friends, my family, you matter. All the people I touch and who touch me back. That's what matters, and the care I take of those relationships is what's important. All the rest of it is just entertainment, diversion. It's not what's at the core of things.

Maybe that's why I'm writing now. My relationship with you has been one of the most important ones in my life. I don't want to abuse this relationship. It's too precious. But maybe I am abusing it by continuing to write to you and keep the connection after I've refused to make a commitment. I would like to keep writing because you are still the only one I can tell certain things to. But I wonder if I'm being selfish.

Please think hard about what I'm saying. If you think we should have some real space between us, write one more time and let me know. If you're sure you can deal with me as a friend, I'll be glad to keep writing. But I don't want to mislead you or hurt you.

I'm going to sign off now. This is the last day I have to use this great camera I've been loaned. I want to make the most of it. I hope you're having a terrific summer. Let me know what you think about everything I've said.

Love, Carrie.

Sticking her letter in her bag, Carrie fished out the camera and got to her feet. Her first photo was of the wildflowers by the bottom step. Their petals were beginning to close, yet they seemed to lean their heads as if to catch the last of the evening sunlight.

Walking along the shore, she spotted an old high-top sneaker someone had left behind. When she got nearer, she was startled by a crab that seemed to have made its home inside it. Quickly she dropped to her stomach, focused, and snapped. She caught the crab with one of its claws sticking up over the top of the sneaker. *That should be a funny picture,* she thought, smiling to herself.

Farther up the shore, someone had drawn a big heart in the sand with a stick. Inside was written *Sonny loves . . .* The name of whomever Sonny loved and the point of the heart had been washed away by the surf. Carrie took a picture of the heart just as the rising tide lapped up a little more of the word *loves*. Carrie decided to title the picture "All Washed Up."

For the next hour, Carrie lost track of time. Everywhere she looked, another photo presented itself to her artistic eye. As the sun sank lower in the sky the light kept changing, creating new challenges, new effects.

At one point she was squatting in the rocky surf, aiming up at a seagull that had landed on a boulder. Her dress was hiked up around her thighs, but it was getting wet anyway. She clicked just as the bird took flight. It would be an even better photo than the one she'd envisioned.

Getting to her feet, she turned and froze. Billy was standing at the shoreline watching her. "Hi," she said finally. "How long have you been there?"

"A few minutes," he admitted. "Claudia told me she thought you'd come down here." He wore jeans and a black T-shirt. His long hair was loose and fluttered slightly in the soft evening breeze that had suddenly come in off the ocean. "You were pretty intent on getting that shot."

"I got it, too," she said with a small smile. "I guess you came to get this," she said, lifting the camera strap from around her neck as she walked toward him. "I wasn't expecting you till later."

As she neared him she realized he was holding something at his side. "Claudia's shoes!" she cried.

He held them out to her. "Here you go, Cinderella," he said. "After I saw you at the beach today we all went over to the studio to put the last touches on the demo. Frank and Pres were horsing around and a drumstick got tossed behind a cabinet. When I went to get it, there were the shoes."

"That's weird," Carrie commented. Maybe they'd gotten kicked there by accident. Or maybe someone had hidden them—someone like Kristy Powell. It didn't really matter anymore. She had the shoes. That was one mistake she could repair.

"Thanks for returning them," she said. She held out the camera to him.

"Okay, well, I'll see you," he said, taking it from her. Carrie watched as he headed for the steps. All of a sudden he turned. "Can I ask you a question, Carrie?"

"Sure."

"Who the hell are you, anyway?"

"What do you mean?" she asked.

"I mean, you keep changing. I had one impression of you, then you come to the party at the studio and you act like some airhead groupie who's hot to trot and can't hold her liquor. The next day you're back to being the girl I was attracted to, but when I ask you out, you do some kind of born-to-be-wild routine on me."

"I guess it must have been pretty confusing," Carrie admitted.

"I had pretty much decided that you were too strange for me. Then I saw you today at the beach and you were back to your old self. All during the studio session I couldn't stop thinking about you. I kept seeing your face the way it looked when you were hugging Chloe and you were crying. You looked really beautiful."

He thought I looked beautiful? At that *moment?*

"You like girls with wet, stringy hair and puffy eyes, huh?" she joked uncomfortably.

"I'm not kidding," he stated.

"I know you're not," she said quietly, kneeling down on her blanket. Billy knelt down beside her. "All right. If you want the whole mortifying truth, here it is," she blurted out. "Around the island I always saw you with these very sexy-looking girls. They come to your shows, they hang all over you. Kristy Powell in particular. I really liked you and I didn't want to lose out because you thought I was just this dumb kid who didn't know anything about life."

To her surprise Billy threw his head back and laughed. "Man, were you wrong!" he said, catching his breath. "After the first time I met you at Wheels, I said to Pres, 'Now there's a good-looking girl you can actually talk to. Not like those other dingbats we're always meeting.'"

"Then I went and turned into a dingbat on you," Carrie realized.

"Yeah, you did," he agreed.

"Why didn't you tell me how you felt sooner?" she asked.

"It's my turn to make a confession. I'm so attracted to you that I wanted to make it work, even if you were kind of strange. It was like I was having this tug-of-war with myself. Part of me said I should forget about you, and another part of me couldn't do it."

"What a mess," Carrie laughed. "You and I sure managed not to communicate. I wish we could start all over again."

"Maybe we can," said Billy as he took her hand in his. Carrie looked deep into his eyes and felt that familiar flutter. Then she looked down, self-conscious. She wanted to take it slowly this time, even though her body was telling her to surge ahead. Billy seemed to catch the awkward feeling, too.

"Well, what about teaching me how to use this camera?" he said huskily.

Carrie looked up. *He really is a nice guy,* she thought, almost surprised. *I feel so comfortable with him. Like I used to before I started acting like a jerk and wrecked it all.*

Carrie might not know how to be a sexpot airhead, but now she didn't want to. She *did* know about cameras, and as she began to explain she felt so comfortable she even forgot to be self-conscious.

"It's pretty automatic," she found herself saying easily. "Composing the picture is probably the most important part of taking a great photo."

Billy sat back and leaned on his elbows. "All right, then, tell me about composition."

Carrie sat up and began explaining elements of basic composition that she'd studied in books. "You want to avoid flatness," she said at one point. She took three rocks and lined them up side by side. "See? That's boring. But now look." She rearranged the rocks, one to the front of another, the third one off to the side and slightly behind. "I've added some depth to the composition, and the same objects are now a lot more visually interesting. A painter can move objects, but a photographer often has to use what's given. So since you can't always move the objects, you have to learn to move yourself into angles that will make your shots more interesting."

"You know what else is interesting?" said Billy, sitting forward.

"What?" she asked.

"You. You're very interesting. I'm glad we're finally talking."

"Me, too," said Carrie, suddenly feeling a little shy. She jumped to her feet. "Come on, I have a few more pictures on this roll. Why don't you take them? The sunset should give you some nice effects."

Billy tried a few shots, asking questions as he went. Carrie realized that she wasn't the only one who had been putting on an act. For the first time, she was seeing the natural, relaxed Billy.

The strong, kind of quiet, sex-symbol persona had fallen away. Underneath was a person with an easy smile and an inquisitive, even delightfully childlike eagerness to explore new things.

It occurred to Carrie that although the rock-star stance had attracted her with its aura of glamor and danger, it wasn't really what she'd responded to in Billy. This person she was seeing now as he fumbled earnestly with the camera, this was the person with whom she'd felt that silent communication.

Now he stood taking a picture of the stairway leading down to the beach. The brilliant sunset had colored the white, weathered wood a warm pink. "That's going to be pretty," she commented, silently impressed with his selection of subject. He could have turned the camera to the spectacular sunset behind him, but instead he chose to shoot its more subtle reflection. There was a lot more to Billy Sampson than she'd thought.

While he set up his shot, Carrie turned out to the water and gazed at the sunset. She had no trouble understanding why they had named this Sunset Island. The sunsets here were nothing short of spectacular. Tonight's was exceptionally so. Golden and pink clouds made a calico pattern across the sky.

Moving directly behind Billy, she tried to envision what he was seeing through his lens. Putting her hands on his side, she gently moved him over a few steps. "You don't want the staircase exactly in the middle. Your picture will look like it's chopped in half. Putting it off center makes it more pleasing to the eye," she explained.

This is a switch, she thought. With Josh, she had always been in the role of student. Josh was an avid reader and a natural teacher. He'd opened up all sorts of interesting subjects for her. Yet it was nice to be the teacher for a change. It made her feel more equal.

Billy took the picture. "You're right, that does look better," he agreed. "That was the last shot, I think," he added, checking the film count.

He turned toward the ocean. "God, this is a beautiful place," he said. "When you're on the beach alone like this, you feel as if the rest of the world doesn't even exist."

Then he gently drew her to him. They seemed to melt together as they wrapped their arms around each other and kissed.

At that moment Carrie knew what he'd been talking about. For her right then there was nothing else in the world. There was only Billy's strong caress and the soft, warm gentleness of his tender kiss.

FOURTEEN

"I don't believe it," squealed Sam. "He actually took you to dinner at the Sunset Inn."

Carrie nodded happily. "He said he owed me a proper first date since we were starting all over again. He even went home and got a sports jacket. But when we got to the restaurant, the maître d' said he had to wear a tie. I figured it was all over then, but Billy didn't argue at all. We jumped in the van and drove down to the Cheap Boutique. Beth was just closing up, but she let us in anyway. We found this great tie with a picture of a dead fish right down the front. The maître d' didn't seem too happy when we came back, but he had to seat us."

"Was it great?" asked Emma dreamily.

"It was the best evening I've ever had in my life," sighed Carrie. And it had been. After the elegant dinner, they'd gone dancing at the Play Café. Everyone wanted Billy's attention, but he had made it clear that he was with Carrie. After that, they'd walked along the ocean, talking and, later, stopping to kiss some more in the light of the full moon.

Now the girls sat on the beach enjoying a few hours off. “See?” said Sam. “I told you a little makeup would work wonders for you.”

“Aaagh!” Carried screamed, holding up her hands as if she were about to strangle Sam. “Billy doesn’t care if I wear makeup or not; he likes me the way I am. Or at least the way I was before you redid me.”

“Hmmmph,” Sam sniffed. “There’s no accounting for taste.” She stretched out her long legs and poured handfuls of warm sand on her ankles. “So when are you going to set up a double date with you guys for me with Pres?”

“Do you really want to?” Carrie asked.

“Oh, no. I have no desire to date a gorgeous hunk of burning love. I must have been out of my mind. Forget I even mentioned it,” Sam cried. “Maybe it’s sunstroke. What could I have been thinking? I must be—”

“All right. Okay,” Carrie laughed. “I was just checking. I’ll ask Billy if he thinks it’s a good idea.”

Sam patted Carrie’s shoulder. “You’re a pal.”

“It’s great to be in love,” sighed Emma, resting her chin on her knees. “I don’t even want to think about September.”

“Things are getting really serious with you and Kurt, aren’t they?” Carrie noticed.

Emma nodded. “You know what he told Lorell about our renting a sailboat and going around the world together? I'm getting the idea that he's more than half-serious."

"Oh, how totally romantic!" said Sam. "Has he actually told you this?"

"No, but he keeps talking about it. He says, 'Wouldn't it be great if we could . . .' but the daydreams are starting to sound more and more real."

"Would you go?" asked Carrie.

"I don't know," Emma replied.

"That's a big choice to have to make," Carrie sympathized. "I was so excited about going to Yale in the fall; now the thought of leaving here gives me a stomachache."

"Would you two relax?" Sam scolded. "July isn't nearly over. Lots of things are going to happen before September. So just chill and enjoy yourselves."

"You're right," Emma agreed, smiling.

Suddenly Sam's hands flew to her chest. "Oh, God!" she whispered dramatically. "I don't believe what I'm seeing. This is too great for words."

Emma and Carrie followed her gaze down the beach. Walking along the waterline were Daphne and Lorell. Daphne looked like a gangly scarecrow with her thin arms jutting out of an oversized T-shirt—but she looked good next to Lorell.

Lorell was wearing the leopard-print-and-mesh suit with the built-up bra. It looked every bit as awful as it had on Carrie. Even more so, since Lorell's figure put her at more of a disadvantage.

"You know, I've often heard my mother talk about outfits that wear you instead of you wearing them," Emma said, giggling. "Now I know what she means." Slim Lorell was all mesh-exposed white flesh and dangerously pointed breasts.

Sam was nearly gasping with hysteria. "I can't believe it really worked," she finally managed.

"I feel a little guilty," said Carrie, laughing nonetheless.

"No you don't," Sam said. "Lorell deserves it."

"I think she does," Emma agreed.

Lorell caught sight of them and waved. Choking down their laughter, they waved back. Lorell spread her arms wide and looked at them with a how-do-you-like-it expression.

Sam stuck her thumb in the air. Emma nodded coolly and Carrie smiled. Tossing her dark hair back proudly, Lorell gestured for Daphne to follow her as they headed on down the beach.

"Oh, there is justice in the world after all," Emma said happily. "That was great."

Sam got to her feet and picked up her tote bag. "I must bid you ladies adieu," she said. "I must go home and prepare for my cocktail rendezvous this evening with Flash Hathaway. I want him to see my modeling potential in its full glory."

"They won't serve you in a bar," Emma pointed out.

"So I won't drink. But I couldn't invite Flash

out for sodas, could I? I mean, it's not exactly the height of sophistication."

"Be careful with him," Carrie warned again.

"No problemo," Sam said glibly. "See you guys later. I'll have a full report."

"I hope she'll be okay," Carrie worried as she watched Sam saunter away on her long legs.

"She will be," Emma assured her. "Sam has more experience with guys than both of us put together." She, too, got up and began gathering her things. "I'm on duty tonight, I'd better get back. Are you coming?"

Carrie shook her head. "No, I'll stay awhile and finish my book. Lately Claudia and Graham are on this spend-time-with-the-kids kick. I want to enjoy my freedom while it lasts."

"Enjoy yourself," Emma said as she left.

Carrie took out her book and opened it. Before she began reading, she gazed out past the crowd of people to the blue waves crashing against the shore. Sam had been right. So much more was still going to happen, she thought. There would be a lot more ups and downs before the summer was over.

But for now she felt happy. Billy and she were together. She still had her job. And most important, she knew herself a little better.

Closing her eyes, she lay back and let the warm sun wash over her. She'd never imagined this summer would turn out to be so wonderful. Especially after its rocky beginning. With a little luck—and Billy at her side—it was only going to get better.